"Let me put it  **Khalil said slo**

dressed.

"The line of successi... ...quite specific. On my thirtieth birthday—in a matter of months—I am to inherit the throne. I will be crowned sheikh, but only if I am married. It is a peculiar requirement of our country's constitution. I have known for a long time that I must choose a bride and marry swiftly. If we were to do this your way and not marry, I still would not permit you to leave Khatrain until the children were born, at which point I would demand that they remain here. In the meantime, I would be forced to marry one of the women my advisers have urged me to consider, and that woman, my wife and sheikha, would be the stepmother to our children. Is that the future you want?"

She gasped, hot, bright lights flashing in her eyes at the awful picture he painted.

"Or," he continued, his voice husky, his accent thick, "you could accept my proposal."

Clare Connelly was raised in small-town Australia among a family of avid readers. She spent much of her childhood up a tree, Harlequin book in hand. Clare is married to her own real-life hero, and they live in a bungalow near the sea with their two children. She is frequently found staring into space—a surefire sign she is in the world of her characters. She has a penchant for French food and ice-cold champagne, and Harlequin novels continue to be her favorite-ever books. Writing for Harlequin Presents is a long-held dream. Clare can be contacted via clareconnelly.com or on her Facebook page.

Books by Clare Connelly

Harlequin Presents

Redemption of the Untamed Italian
The Secret Kept from the King
Hired by the Impossible Greek
Their Impossible Desert Match
My Forbidden Royal Fling

A Billion-Dollar Singapore Christmas

An Heir Claimed by Christmas

No Strings Christmas
(Available from Harlequin DARE)

Signed, Sealed...Seduced

Cinderella's Night in Venice

Visit the Author Profile page
at Harlequin.com for more titles.

Clare Connelly

CROWNED FOR HIS DESERT TWINS

HARLEQUIN
PRESENTS

Recycling programs
for this product may
not exist in your area.

ISBN-13: 978-1-335-56899-1

Crowned for His Desert Twins

Copyright © 2021 by Clare Connelly

All rights reserved. No part of this book may be used or reproduced in
any manner whatsoever without written permission except in the case of
brief quotations embodied in critical articles and reviews.

This is a work of fiction. Names, characters, places and incidents
are either the product of the author's imagination or are used fictitiously.
Any resemblance to actual persons, living or dead, businesses,
companies, events or locales is entirely coincidental.

This edition published by arrangement with Harlequin Books S.A.

For questions and comments about the quality of this book,
please contact us at CustomerService@Harlequin.com.

Harlequin Enterprises ULC
22 Adelaide St. West, 40th Floor
Toronto, Ontario M5H 4E3, Canada
www.Harlequin.com

Printed in U.S.A.

CROWNED FOR HIS DESERT TWINS

To Trish Morey, for your wisdom, kindness and hours of fabulous stories.

PROLOGUE

THE ROOM SWARMED with exactly the sort of people Khalil had come to think of as 'the usual suspects' at such events. The ballroom of the elegant Manhattan hotel buzzed with America's elite, women in ball gowns and men in suits, chattering non-stop so the noise was like the buzz of cicadas droning on incessantly.

'Your Highness?' A waiter approached nervously, holding a stainless-steel tray and a single glass of Scotch.

Khalil's lips twisted cynically. Even here, across the other side of the world, his reputation preceded him. The Ruthless Prince, he thought with a sneer. Had he always been regarded as such? Or was it just after Fatima, when it had become easier to see people as they truly were, and therefore harder to hide his contempt? He lifted the glass with a dismissive nod, and the waiter scuttled away gratefully.

It was strong and spiced with citrus, just as

he liked it. He took a sip, his eyes travelling the room, quirking a brow in greeting as he recognised a familiar face in conversation near the entrance, before his gaze continued to roam, his features unknowingly bearing an expression of bored impatience. This had never been his scene. He much preferred the important parts of ruling—policy, education, funding, policing. The frothy parties and socialising were a pointless waste of time, time he simply didn't have. Drawing himself to his full six and a half feet, he looked towards a set of wide doors, preparing to escape this pointless event, having at least made an appearance to appease international diplomatic relations.

And then, he saw her.

His gaze arrested, his body straightened unconsciously, something like adrenaline filled his mouth as he stared at the most beautiful woman he'd ever seen. Tall and slender with blonde hair that was pinned into a bun low on her nape, she wore a deep blue gown that demanded attention—not for the dress so much as for what it did to her figure. Curved breasts and hips, a slim waist and long legs were encased in a sheath of fabric that, while elegant enough to meet the dress code, lacked the puffy confection of the ball gowns the other women wore. Her smile was quick and transformed her face, showing dimples in either cheek, so her eyes looked as though they were filled with glitter.

Throwing back the rest of his Scotch, already poised to move closer, Khalil moved his attention to encompass her date almost as an afterthought. Whoever it was, it didn't matter. Such considerations were irrelevant to Sheikh Khalil el Abdul, ruler to one of the most prosperous countries in the Middle East. No woman he'd ever wanted had resisted him; it didn't occur to him she might be the first.

The blonde smiled again and Khalil's eyes narrowed, looking to the recipient of this beautiful gift. The man's back was turned to him, so all Khalil could tell was that he was fair and stood about a foot shorter than Khalil, almost the same height as the woman. He wore a tuxedo with tails, his shoes polished. But it was when the man angled his face in profile that a blade cut through Khalil's chest.

The recognition was instantaneous. He never forgot a face, but this one in particular he had good cause to recollect—and despise. Ethan Graves, his one-time friend, a man he'd thought well enough of to introduce to his cousin—more like a sister, really—a man who'd then gone on to destroy Astrid's life. A familiar rush of guilt churned through him. He couldn't look at Ethan without seeing Astrid—the way their relationship had affected her. If only he hadn't set them up! If only he'd seen what was happening before it was too late…

Khalil squeezed the Scotch glass so hard it almost broke. He put it down before he cracked it, and eyed the pair with renewed interest.

His heart was beating hard, determination moving through his veins like steel. There was no one on earth he hated more than he did Ethan Graves. The man was the lowest of the low. He'd be doing this woman a favour by seducing her away from Ethan. Ethan wasn't good enough for the air he breathed, let alone for this woman to be giving him her attention.

Yes, she would benefit from this plan too but, mainly, Khalil wanted to make Ethan suffer. He wanted to hurt him; he'd been hoping for a chance to avenge his cousin, and fate had delivered that opportunity right into his lap. Adrenaline burst through him, determination wiping anything else from his mind.

He hated Ethan Graves, and there was nothing he wouldn't do to make the other man pay, including seducing his very beautiful lover…

CHAPTER ONE

'IN A ROOM full of peacocks, you are the only exotic bird.'

The voice whispered against her cheek, words murmured from behind, his accent spiced, tone deep. The flesh on India's arms lifted in a fine covering of goosebumps even before she'd turned around to see who was speaking to her. His appearance didn't help matters. She'd expected another boring banker type, dressed to the nines and swelled up with their own importance, and instead she'd come face to face with—

But it was impossible to put into words the effect of this man's beauty. He was tall and broad, with swarthy skin and dark hair that brushed his collar, a slight kick at the bottom. His brows were thick and dark, his bone structure symmetrical, his jawline square, covered with stubble, his lips generous and wide, his nose straight and long. He had eyes that were like never-ending tunnels, deep and fascinating, flecked with brown and black and gold, rimmed in thick, dark lashes that gave him the appearance of wearing eyeliner. She stared up at him breathlessly, completely unprepared for this, almost forgetting where she was and what she was doing.

But the amnesia was temporary.

India was working, and she couldn't afford to do anything to mess up this job—or any job—so she blinked, pushing her features into a politely dismissive smile. 'Thank you,' she murmured, turning her attention back to the bar just in time to see another woman—one of the peacocks this man had alluded to—sweeping in front of her and grabbing the barman's attention.

'Damn it,' she muttered under her breath.

'What is it you would like to drink?' His voice was like treacle—completely smooth and addictive. She bit back an irrational desire to suggest he could have a second career as an audiobook narrator, because if this man was here, at this thousand-dollars-a-head charity event, it was unlikely he was in need of a supplemental income.

'It's fine,' she dismissed. 'I'm next in line.'

'You were next in line before too,' he pointed out.

She slid him a glance. 'Yes, and if you hadn't distracted me, I would have ordered by now.'

In response, his lips curled in a smile of undisguised appreciation. 'Allow me,' he murmured, putting a hand in the small of her back and drawing her closer to him. Shocked, her body moved without her brain's consent, so her side connected with his, and she startled, her eyes leaping to his in surprise as sparks flared beneath her skin. Somehow, he found a small gap at the front of the bar and moved them towards it, lifting a hand at the same time.

To India's surprise, a waitress appeared immediately. 'Good evening, sir.' She dipped her head forward deferentially, so India's gaze flicked back to the stranger's face. 'May I get you a drink?'

'The lady would like to order,' he said, his fingers moving gently over her back now, the pattern he was drawing there rhythmic and distracting, so that when India opened her mouth to speak her voice emerged stilted.

'A mineral water for me, please, but in a champagne flute, and a glass of pinot noir.'

'And for you, Your Highness?' The waitress looked up at him.

India startled once more. *Your Highness?* The man's eyes caught hers, amusement in those never-ending depths, and embarrassment curdled her belly. Was he enjoying her surprise? The fact she had no idea who he was? No doubt he moved in these circles all the time, whereas India was an occasional guest, when the agency was in a jam and had to send her on a blue-chip date—

usually reserved for the escorts who'd worked at the agency the longest. Her tenure was only new—twelve months ago the bottom had fallen out of her world, and she'd been doing whatever she could to make ends meet since then. She'd do whatever was necessary to keep her beloved younger brother in college. He'd already lost so much; she wouldn't allow him to lose his degree as well.

'A mineral water as well, but not in a champagne flute.'

'Your *Highness*?' India queried, while the waitress disappeared to prepare their drinks.

'Yes?'

She narrowed her gaze. 'You're royalty?'

'It would appear so.'

'Are you being deliberately secretive?'

'That's something I've never been called before.'

'Perhaps not to your face.'

He laughed then, a rich sound that had more than one head turning in their direction and which set India's pulse into overdrive. Not just her pulse. Every cell in her body was trembling with awareness, and she was secretly glad that the crowd pushing towards the bar meant they were being jostled closer together, her body shifting nearer to his big, broad frame until they were touching.

'Who are you?' she repeated, curiosity spreading through her.

'My name is Khalil,' he said.

'But should I call you "Your Highness"?'

'No, that would not be appropriate.'

Her brow furrowed in confusion. 'But if you're a king…?'

'I am not yet a king,' he said, half dismissively, so she wondered if she'd said the wrong thing somehow. But then he was moving closer, his head lowering to her ear, so he could whisper against her flesh. 'And I would like to hear my name on your lips, rather than my title.'

It was just a throwaway comment, and yet something about the way he'd phrased it and the timbre of his voice set her nerves jangling. A slick of heat flooded her body, low in her abdomen, so she was conscious of the way her nipples strained against the soft silk of her dress. She wasn't wearing a bra—she didn't possess one that worked with the lines of the dress—and so her breasts were crushed against the hard warmth of his chest, every nerve-ending tantalisingly aware of his proximity and raw charisma.

His eyes flicked to her mouth and her lips parted as if by magic, her heart rate as fast as if she'd just run a marathon. Her lips tingled all over. She was overcome with sensations she'd never known before. Surrounded by the crush of New York's elite and somewhere, only a few feet away, the date who was paying handsomely for her time, all she could think of was the man before her.

'Khalil,' she said, as if to stir herself from the strange dream that was wrapping tentacles around her.

His eyes flared with unmistakable desire. Her stomach swooped. 'And your name?' The question was said with a tone of command.

'I-India,' she stammered for the first time in years, since a speech pathologist had helped her overcome the childhood impediment.

'India.' His hand shifted to her hip, holding her close to him, promising things she desperately wanted to experience. 'It is a pleasure to meet you.'

'Here are your drinks, sir, ma'am.' The waitress's appearance was a welcome interruption. India's eyes flared wide and she would have stood back a little, if she could have. But there were too many people crowding around them, so India told herself she had no choice but to stay right where she was: for now—it was a convenient excuse, because she didn't really want to put any space between them anyway.

'Leave them on the bar.' He didn't take his eyes off India's face. She felt warm and desirable, and a thousand kinds of need. 'Tell me about yourself.'

India blinked, she'd never been asked this question, not on any of the agency dates she'd attended in the past year.

'I suspect it would be far more interesting if you told me about yourself,' she said truthfully, ignoring the glass of pinot noir to her right—due to be delivered to her date at any moment.

'Why is that?'

'Well, you're the first royal I've ever met,' she said with a lift of one shoulder. It drew his gaze downwards, and from the creamy flesh of her shoulder sideways, to the exposed decolletage and valley between her breasts. India sucked in a sharp breath, butterflies colonising her belly. His interest was unmistakable, but her own physical response bowled her over.

'And you are the first woman named India I have ever met. What is your point?'

Her cheeks flooded with warmth. She was heart-stoppingly attracted to him, and that was a disaster. Or, at the very least, hugely inconvenient, because she was on a date with a client and she wasn't being paid to flirt with another man. She could imagine the complaint Ethan— who seemed as if he had definite jerk potential— would make to the agency if he saw her locked in intimate conversation with another man—

particularly one like this. She couldn't say why she knew that *this* man in particular would be incendiary, except that he was so hyper-masculine. She suspected he was intimidating to all other males.

And very likely knew it.

'My point…' she pulled away from him with difficulty, curling her fingers around the drinks '…is that I should think your life story would outdo mine any day.' She offered him a small smile. 'But unfortunately, I can't stay to hear it. I'm here with someone.'

His eyes flashed with an emotion she couldn't decipher. Annoyance? Impatience? Irritation?

She understood all three. But her work was hugely important—she'd already spent tonight's pay cheque three times over, and the very thought of the college-fee notice stuck to the fridge door had her breaking out in a cold sweat.

'Someone you'd prefer to be with?' he prompted with easy confidence. What must it have been like to be so self-assured? Oh, he was right, of course. She'd have given anything to swap out her dates, but this was business, not pleasure, and so her own needs had to take a back seat.

It wasn't a fair question. 'I came here with someone else.'

'It does not follow you must leave with him, *azeezi*.'

'Actually, it does.' She flicked a glance downwards, regret in her heart. On this night, of all nights—her twenty-fourth birthday—what she wouldn't have given to indulge her own wants, just for once! The day had been so lonely, in stark contrast to the way her mother, stepfather and brother used to make a fuss each year. Oh, Jackson had still called, and they'd spoken for almost an hour—his happiness had lifted her heart for a time. But beyond that, it was just India in a big, empty home, thinking of the family she'd used to have, the way things used to be. Flirting with this incredibly handsome stranger would have been the perfect present to herself, but what she needed, more than anything, was the payment for tonight. She couldn't do anything to risk the job. With true remorse, she offered him a parting smile. 'It was nice to meet you, Your Highness.'

But he wasn't ready to let it go. 'I asked you to call me Khalil,' he reminded her softly. His thumb pressed beneath her chin, lifting her face to his, so their eyes locked and the world seemed to disappear, tipping away, leaving just the two of them on a precipice of time and space.

'I can't call you anything,' she said, her voice lacking the firmness she needed despite her resolve. 'I must go.'

'Is it what you want?'

'Don't keep asking me that.'

'Have I already?'

'More or less.' She sighed, but didn't look away. 'My date will be waiting for me.'

Now his lips curled with unmistakable derision. 'A date who sent you to the bar to get his drink? Is such a man really worthy of your time?'

'I offered,' she said. 'He was in an important business conversation.'

'No conversation is more important than your time. If you were here with me, you would know that.'

Her lips parted; a reply was impossible.

'A man lucky enough to secure a date with you should make it his life's mission to keep you happy, not send you scurrying to the bar whenever he develops a thirst.'

Her breath escaped in a hot rush. 'It's not—like that—' she insisted. Her pulse was thready and her lips were tingling. Even as she acknowledged that Ethan had, in fact, pointed to the bar and given her his order, treating her like the paid companion she, in fact, was.

'Would you like to hear what a date with me would entail?'

'I have to get back,' she groaned huskily, without making any attempt to free herself from his proximity.

'First, I would send you the address of a Fifth Avenue boutique, so you could go and enjoy choosing what you would wear—lingerie, a dress, shoes, jewellery, anything your heart desired. My driver would then take you to the presidential suite at the Carlisle, where you would spend the afternoon preparing, pampering and, most vitally, enjoying a nap to be sure you were well rested.'

A frisson of desire ran the length of her spine at the image he was painting. It was a far cry from the life she currently led.

'I would collect you at eight. We would go for dinner, but I would book the entire restaurant to be sure we each had the other's full attention. Alone, we would dance with no eyes on us, and then, before midnight, we would return to your hotel room, where I would enjoy hearing my name on your lips over, and over, and over again.'

Her eyes closed as imagery flourished in her brain, his body naked, hers, entangled in billion-thread-count sheets at the impossibly prestigious hotel. The night sounded like perfection, and if India hadn't learned for herself how fleeting men's interest would be, then she might not have known to ask the next question. But once bitten, twice shy, was a motto that had served India well for years.

'And in the morning?' she whispered, the thickness to her voice betraying how tempted she was by his words.

Her eyes glanced at his, just in time to see a spark of something like surprise in their depths.

'The morning would be a new day,' he said quietly.

'And without you in it.'

His head dipped forward. 'I am never in America for long. My life is in Khatrain.'

Ah! Khatrain. She knew of the country instantly, of course. Prosperous, modern, politically important, perched on the edge of the Persian Gulf with a capital city that was one of the modern wonders of the world.

'The date sounds wonderful,' she said wistfully. 'But I make it a rule not to get involved in one-night stands.' Now she pulled backwards, but not quickly enough.

'Even when it's what you want?' he prompted silkily.

Her heart began to slam into her ribs. She stared up at him, lost in his eyes, his nearness, her breath burning. 'How do you know what I want?'

'I don't. I'm guessing. Am I wrong?'

Yes. Say yes. But India was honest to a fault. She shook her head once, her body swaying forward.

'I didn't think so,' he said simply, his head dropping slowly to hers, his eyes teasing her, tempting her. He intended to kiss her, and even when India knew she should pull away, her body moved of its own volition, her feet pushing her higher, willingly submitting to his passionate kiss, his outright possession, so her ability to think was blown completely to smithereens.

His hand stroked her hip, and one leg shifted, moving forward to brace her, forming a sort of cage around her body, holding her just where she was, totally wrapped up in him. 'It would only be one night, but the night would set your soul on fire, *azeezi*, I promise.'

It was like being doused in ice water. She jerked her face away, quickly looking towards the crowded bar. Ethan's back was turned to her—thank God. Her fingertips quivered with the flood of sensations and the rush of anxiety over what had just happened. She'd be fired for sure if Ethan reported this to the agency, and she couldn't live with that. Where else would she get a job like this? Warm Engagements was an escort agency with a difference—no sex between client and staff. It was a hard rule, and it meant India felt safe accepting bookings without worrying that her client was going to expect a little 'added service' at the end of the night, and it paid ten times better than anything else she was even remotely qualified for.

'I can't,' she said, her eyes awash with anguish because, oh, how she wanted to! 'Please, just, forget we ever met.'

CHAPTER TWO

ETHAN'S VOICE HAD been droning on for a very, very long time. India nodded and smiled—it was pretty obvious he didn't require much more than that. The few times she'd attempted to interject her own thoughts, he'd given her a condescending look, as if to imply, 'what would you know about it?' and then waffled on some more. His companions didn't seem to mind, which led India to believe that Ethan Graves was either seriously rich or seriously important. There was no other reason for so many people to be intent on sucking up to him. Oh, he was handsome, in that movie star way, but he was clearly so full of himself that India was beyond bored.

Unfortunately, that left her brain with way, way too much run time, and it was occupied on a singular task: overthinking the experience she'd had with Khalil—she didn't even know his last name! And yet he'd almost kissed her as though she were his dying breath, and he had—for that moment—been all she was aware of. She tried to think of other matters. Her conversation with Jackson this morning, for example, and how happy he'd sounded, his placement at college coming at a time when he'd been besieged by grief—they both had been—after the sudden, tragic loss of their parents. Her life's purpose had become, in the last twelve months, about maintaining the status quo for him.

She owed that to her mother and stepfather. She'd loved them so much, and they'd worked so hard to give their children a great life. She'd do anything she could to honour them, and working out a way to cover Jackson's expensive tuition so he could take up his place at the prestigious institution seemed like a good place to start. They'd been so proud when he'd got his acceptance letter. Jackson's degree had meant the world to them. She had to make sure he was able to complete his studies.

But was it tenable? Could she keep this up for another three years? Panic rose in her chest, as it always did when she contemplated the future, the financial obligations around her neck tightening until she felt as though she were going to black out. Unfortunately, there were only so many ways an unqualified twenty-four-year-old could make money in this economy, and the amount of money India required meant she'd had no option but to turn to a job like this. Escorting wealthy men to fancy functions wasn't exactly her dream career, but it paid well. And Jackson was worth it.

She would have done anything she could to be with him today. It was her first birthday without her parents. They'd died three days after she turned twenty-three. She hadn't stopped to think about that, but this morning, she'd faced this milestone without them, and it had brought all the grief and loneliness and missing them back so she'd wished the day away, simply so she could get this 'first' day over with. Christmas had been the same. Jackson had come home though, so at least they'd been together, but it had been hollow and haunting, their parents' absence making the holiday heavy with sadness.

Ethan's companions laughed at something he'd said, dragging her back to the conversation. She faked a laugh, before lifting the mineral water to her lips and taking a sip. It wasn't intentional, but her eyes shifted sideways and it was like being electric-shocked.

Khalil stood across the room, in a conversation he clearly wasn't listening to. His eyes bored into her in a way that sent her pulse into overdrive. She didn't—couldn't—look away, and a moment later his lip lifted in a knowing smile, before his eyes dipped lower, undertaking a slower, more thorough inspection. Her body's response was immediate. Her stomach squeezed and her breasts tingled, her nipples taut. She knew he realised, and heat bloomed in her cheeks. India sipped her drink again then forced herself to listen to Ethan, dragging her gaze back to her client.

He knew nothing about economics. He clearly thought he did, but India had finished two years of her degree and, beyond that, economics had long been a passion of hers. She knew that he was fudging numbers and his understanding of trade relationships was deeply warped. Did the others in the group realise?

On he went, for at least another twenty minutes, before turning to India. 'Darling, would you mind fetching me another from the bar?'

Heat flushed her cheeks for a different reason now, and a quick glance confirmed that Khalil was watching, a look in his eyes that knocked the breath from her lungs.

'Of course not,' she said, embarrassed, but all too aware she was being paid to be the perfect date.

'Anyone else for a drink?' he offered the group.

'A beer,' one of the men said with a grin of appreciation.

'Same,' another agreed.

India smiled through gritted teeth as she turned and walked towards the bar.

'You know, there are waiters here who would

happily take care of his needs for you.' Khalil was behind her, his voice caressing. 'Why does he send you like a little servant?'

The moment he spoke, she realised she'd been hoping he would pursue her. 'I'm his date and I'm happy to make him happy.'

'Is this what you think a date should be like?' Khalil murmured, making a tsking sound of disapproval. 'What fools you must have been wasting your time on.'

'You don't know the half of it,' she muttered, before she could stop herself.

'Then let tonight be the night your poor taste in men stops,' he said with a lift of his brow.

'We've already discussed that. I'm not going home with you.'

'Because you'd rather go home with him? Or because I was honest about what would happen the morning after?'

Her heart felt as though she had a stitch. 'A little of both.'

'I don't believe you. Not on the first count. I have been watching you all night and there is no spark between the two of you. Not like when I touch you.'

India swallowed quickly. She'd never felt *anything* like she had when Khalil had touched her, let alone when he'd moved in to kiss her, as though her lips had been designed to dance with his.

'I wish you'd *stop* watching me,' she murmured quietly, except it was a lie. Even his eyes, from across the room, had the power to turn her blood to lava.

'I can't. For as long as you are in this room, I will watch you, and I will want you.'

It was so direct! India's eyes leaped to his, all the breath whooshing out of her. 'Khalil,' she moaned. 'You have to stop this.'

'When it is so obvious that we both want the same thing?'

She couldn't deny that, so she stuck with the line she'd already given him. 'I'm here on a date. I'm not going to ditch him for someone I've just met, okay?'

His response was to reach down and put an arm around her waist, drawing her away from the bar.

'Hey,' she protested. 'I have to order their drinks.'

'Drinks, plural?' He swore under his breath. 'You are retrieving beverages for the entire group?'

'Just a few, it's no big deal.' She waved her hand in the air. 'I offered.'

It was obvious he didn't believe the lie. His lips compressed in an angry slash as he lifted a hand and beckoned another waitress with enviable ease.

'What is your order?' he commanded, and for a moment she was struck dumb by the sheer authority he exuded from every pore of his body, his comfort with command unmistakable.

'India,' he insisted.

She nodded, regathering her wits. 'Um…a pinot noir, and two beers, please.'

'Deliver them to that group, over there. With the arrogant blond man holding forth on matters about which he knows little.'

Her eyes flew to Khalil's face. How did he know? Had he had the misfortune to be stung by Ethan in the past?

She didn't get a chance to ask. Order handed over to a waitress, Khalil was whisking her further away from the bar, towards the edge of the room. There were floor-to-ceiling windows here, bracketed on either side by a plush velvet curtain made of gold damask. Security guards, indiscernible from the tuxedo-clad guests, except for the little earpieces they wore, stood at each window.

As Khalil approached, one of the guards bowed before stepping back. Another pressed the windows, so India realised they were actually French doors, opening onto a narrow balcony that formed a perimeter around the Manhattan high rise.

The view was eye-watering. Picture perfect, showcasing the glittering city in all its postcard glory. Even now, as someone who'd seen the view many times, she felt a rush of emotions as she contemplated the beauty of the outlook.

'That's better,' he remarked, right beside her, his body so close they were almost touching.

She shivered, not because she was cold but because alone out here she experienced a rush of feelings and they were sending her nervous system into overdrive.

Nonetheless, Khalil shrugged out of his jacket, handing it to her on autopilot, so some part of her responded to his ingrained good manners. It reminded her of her stepdad, and the way he'd always treated her mother. But she couldn't think of her parents now—it was too sad. Even a year on from their sudden deaths, and the fallout from that tragedy, tears were still too quick to moisten her eyes.

'I can't stay long,' she said, and heard the acquiescence in her voice as he did. She was fighting him as best she could, but it was a losing battle, given that he was right: she wanted to go home with him, to hell with the fact it would never be more than a one-night stand.

'Why are you so adamant you want to be with him? Is it serious between the two of you?'

She hesitated a moment. 'No, it's not.'

'Surely you can see he's not worth your time?'

'That's none of your business.'

'Isn't it?'

'Khalil.' Her voice was lightly pleading. 'You seem to be forgetting we've just met.'

'I'm not forgetting that. Nor am I forgetting how much I'm looking forward to getting to know you properly.'

Her skin flushed all over. 'You're talking about sex.'

His laugh was a warm reward. 'I'm talking about a long, beautiful night together.'

Desire flashed through her—she wanted that. Oh, she wanted it more than she'd ever wanted anything in her entire life. But how could she? It was so outside her experience... 'I'm sure you do this kind of thing all the time, but I really don't,' she said, brutally honest. 'I know that being here, dressed like this, you might think I'm the kind of woman who...who...'

'Who what?' He pushed, but the smile on his face was teasing her innocence and she hated that! She squared her shoulders and fixed him with a cool glance.

'There's no need to laugh at me.'

He sobered, shaking his head. 'I'm not, I assure you. It's only that I find your honesty refreshing.' An emotion crossed his eyes, a look that made no sense. Guilt? Regret? 'Come home with me.' His voice was gruff. 'We can have coffee, sit and talk if you would prefer. This does not need to be about sex.'

Her lips parted in surprise at the offer. She rejected it instantly. 'Coffee' wasn't enough. She wanted so much more.

'Kiss me properly.' She blurted the command out. Foolish? Definitely. But when he kissed her, she saw things with a blinding clarity—or perhaps it was simply that she stopped overthinking everything, and could truly comprehend what she wanted.

Khalil did not need to be asked twice. He stepped forward, his powerful frame pressing hers back against the brick wall, his body dwarfing hers despite the fact India wasn't short. He was all hard planes and angles, the weight of him against her a pleasure she could barely process. Just like before, he stared into her eyes and dropped his head slowly, giving her time to rethink this, to change her mind, but India had already decided what she wanted.

He sensed her acquiescence, his kiss relentless, his tongue lashing hers as his mouth moved, so she could barely breathe, and yet she kissed him back just as hard with a matching urgency, her hands curving around behind him, her nails digging into his suit jacket with the strength of her desperation.

The dress was a fine silk and his fingers caught the hem, lifting it at one side, so the flimsy evening air brushed her bare legs, creating the perfect contrast to his warmth and hardness. Higher and higher he drew the dress, until his fingers were on her hip, the dress bunched in his palm, and she moaned, low in her throat, because she wanted now to be naked for him, to be all his, just as he'd promised he'd make her.

The thought should have been sobering and yet it wasn't, it was the exact opposite. An erotic fever had overtaken India completely, she was subject to its whims completely.

Higher and higher his hands went, until the dress was at her breasts. She moaned, lights bright behind her eyelids. He broke their kiss so he could stare at her nakedness, his eyes fixated on her in a way that sent a rush of power through her limbs, before his dark head swooped down and his mouth drew one of her nipples in. His teeth clamped down and she cried out, the sharp pleasure too much to bear, more than anything she'd ever experienced. Her body was quivering with needs; the heat between her legs demanded attention.

'Please,' she whimpered, tilting her head back to stare at the sky.

'Say my name,' he demanded, transferring his mouth to her other nipple. She groaned, the touch so perfect, the first breast he'd lavished with attention enjoying the contrast of the cool night air, sending her pulse into overdrive.

'Please, Khalil,' she said instinctively, not even sure what she was asking for, only that her life might very well depend on it.

His wolfish grin when he looked up at her was all the confirmation she needed. Her heart thumped and her stomach rolled with desire. She wanted him; she had to have him.

But it wasn't so easy. There was Ethan to consider—not for himself, but for the fact he was a client and she desperately couldn't afford to lose her job.

'How long are you in town for?' She whimpered, as his hand found her inner thigh and teased the flesh there, tantalisingly close to— and yet desperately far from—her sex.

'Why?' He moved his mouth back to hers, kissing her once more, so answering was impossible. The dress fell back down and she moaned, because the silk against her taut, overly sensitive breasts was a form of torture.

Now his knee wedged her legs apart and she pressed down, her most intimate cluster of nerves seeking gratification, needing a pleasure only he could give her. His laugh was a rumble in his throat, and his fingers worked her hair, loosening it from the bun so it fell in waves down her back.

'Tomorrow night,' she said breathlessly, unable to think beyond the words she was trying to get out. 'A date.'

'No. Tonight.'

'I—'

'Do not tell me you can't,' he said firmly, and she heard his regal authority and knew that, in his country, Khalil would be obeyed by all he met, without question.

'I can't,' she whispered.

'And yet you will, if you want me to make love to you.' And with that, he stepped back, the ultimatum delivered at the same time he put space between them, the distance between their bodies a form of torture for India. She groaned as she straightened, staring at him with disbelief.

'Why?' It was thick with surprise. 'Why does it have to be tonight?'

'Do you think I would accept you going home with another man now?' he said seriously, but with such a sense of possession that her stomach burst into flames. 'You will be mine tonight, India. Not his.'

India knew better than to tell him she wasn't 'anyone's' to claim—she was a sentient human being with her own will and desires—but he knew that already, because he'd stoked her desires to a fever pitch and was currently demanding she exercise her own free will by choosing him over Ethan. He was making her acknowledge their connection, but she was under no illusions: this decision was hers. He was waiting for her answer.

'But how?' she said with a shake of her head. 'I don't want to offend Ethan.'

His eyes narrowed. 'A man who treats you as little more than a waitress deserves to be offended,' he said with firm disapproval, so she smiled despite the precariousness of her situation.

'I'm serious,' she said after a beat. 'We can't be seen leaving together.'

He shrugged. 'Fine. Then tell him you are not well and make your escape. I will follow a short time later.'

Her breath grew thin, as though the altitude were affecting her. Yes, *that* was an option. She could make her excuses via text message, apologising and saying she'd suddenly become unwell. It was hardly a glorious way to conclude the evening, but it also wasn't likely to get her fired.

'Okay,' she said with a quick nod, before she could change her mind. 'Where shall we meet?'

His smile was pure arrogance—as though he'd known all along it would reach this point.

'My car is out the front. I'll let my driver know to expect you.'

A tremor ran down her spine as their plans took a firm shape. There was no turning back;

this was happening. But India didn't want to turn backwards anyway. For this night, and just this night, she wanted to look forward, at the man opposite her, who'd promised to make love to her until she couldn't think straight.

'Fine, I'll meet you soon,' she said.

She turned to leave but he grabbed her hand, pulling her abruptly back to him and kissing her soundly, so her senses were in overdrive all over again.

'Be quick, India. I don't want to wait.'

India nodded, then slipped through the glass doors, into the buzzing ballroom. It took on an almost psychedelic quality now: the world was tilting at an odd angle; her experience with Khalil had sent her into another dimension. She made a beeline for the restrooms, ignoring the queue of Manhattan socialites waiting for a stall to free up and instead heading for a mirror. She braced her palms against the marble counter and stared at her flushed reflection and wild hair. There was no way she could face Ethan like this—even if she wanted to. Surely anyone would take one look at her and know exactly what she'd just been doing!

Pulling her phone from her bag, she loaded up a text message. She'd exchanged a few messages with Ethan to arrange the date, so had his number.

I'm so sorry, but I'm not feeling at all well. I didn't want to interrupt your conversation, nor to risk making you ill. Thank you for a lovely evening.

'Holy hell, what are *you* doing here?'

Khalil couldn't hide the sneer from his face. He hated this man but, until now, he hadn't realised that he'd been waiting a long time for the perfect opportunity to take his revenge. He had fantasised about making Ethan pay for what he'd done to Astrid, he just hadn't known the perfect plan would land right in his lap. He curled his hand into a fist, dug deep into his pocket. For Astrid, he would have liked to punch him hard in that arrogant, pretty-boy face. For India, he wanted to shove him out of the nearest window. What the hell had she seen in this guy?

Khalil clenched his jaw, staring down at the inferior specimen, as the men Ethan had been standing with ebbed away, sensing an impending dispute.

'I was invited,' he drawled. 'And you, Ethan? Looking to find the next wealthy heiress you can sink your teeth into?'

'There's no need.' Ethan's smile was the last word in smarmy. 'My divorce settlement from your cousin was more than enough to set me up for life. I must thank you again for introducing us. You really made all this possible for me.'

Khalil's temper was rock steady, except where his cousin was involved. Orphaned at only a few months old, she'd come to live with Khalil and was more like a little sister to him. There was nothing he wouldn't do to protect her, and, in this instance, avenge her. And appease your own guilt, a little voice reminded him, and of course that was true.

'Now, if you don't mind, I'm going to go and find my date.' Ethan's leering smile at Khalil was the last straw.

'Do you mean India?' For the briefest moment, he regretted the words. India deserved better than this—to become collateral damage in his need for revenge. But he was also saving her from a future with this bastard. Maybe she'd even thank him one day.

Ethan stopped walking, his back straight, as he turned slowly to face Khalil. 'How did you—?' Ethan frowned. 'Do you know her?'

'We've just met, but I intend to know her a lot better.'

'You can't be serious,' Ethan demanded, looking around, his face puce with outrage. A moment later, his phone buzzed and the blond man drew it from his pocket, his eyes darting with unmistakable anger as he read the text message.

She'd messaged him, rather than said goodbye? A small smile touched Khalil's lips at the slightly anxious gesture. Ethan was disappearing into the recesses of his mind, barely worth his time.

'I'm very serious,' Khalil murmured, leaning closer, his expression showing exactly why the press had nicknamed him the Ruthless Prince. 'So while you are alone tonight, you can imagine India and me, together. Believe me when I tell you she won't be missing you at all, Ethan. I'll make sure of that.'

CHAPTER THREE

'MADAM.' A SUITED driver stood waiting, the door to a black car with darkly tinted windows held open, his eyes focussed behind India.

She bit down on her lip, a hint of apprehension at what she was about to do assailing her. But it was too late to turn back, and besides, she didn't want to. Sliding into the car, she realised that it was far larger than an ordinary vehicle, though not quite as big as a limousine. A bench seat was at the back, and, directly opposite, two large chairs faced her, with a shiny black box between them. She took a seat on the bench, knowing it was because she hoped he would sit beside her, wanting to pick up right where they'd left off. The door clicked shut and she sat, hands clasped in her lap, waiting, her heart pounding, her breath burning with the desire he'd invoked.

Her phone beeped and she pulled it out of her bag, guiltily reading the response from Ethan.

I hope you feel better tomorrow, India. Sleep tight.

She winced, not liking how it felt to lie, the unusual turn of events pushing her to act in a seriously uncharacteristic manner. Before she could slide her phone away, it beeped again. A text from Jackson.

Hope you're having a great birthday. Wish I could have been there.

Her heart skipped a beat, because she *was* having a great birthday, and with a hint of disloyalty she realised she was now glad Jackson hadn't come back to New York. She was glad she'd been here tonight, that she'd met Khalil.

Having a great night, miss you. Thanks for checking in. x

She pushed the phone into her bag as the car door opened once more and Khalil stepped in, his frame instantly making the enormous vehicle feel smaller.

'Hi,' she murmured shyly. His cheeks were slashed with colour and his jaw was locked, as though angry or stressed. But as he looked at her he smiled, a smile that sent a kaleidoscope of butterflies into her stomach and pulled an answering smile across her own lips.

'I believe you promised me a life story,' he reminded her as he took the seat beside her, just as she'd hoped.

He pushed his arm up behind the seat, making no effort to keep any kind of space between them.

'I'm not sure you're remembering accurately.' The car's engine throbbed to life. A moment later, a dark screen slid between the back of the car and the front, offering privacy.

'Are you keeping secrets?'

She shook her head, wide-eyed, and lifted a hand to his chest. 'No, I just—'

But he understood. His eyes flared as he dipped his head lower. 'Don't want to talk?' He finished the sentence for her, brushing his lips over hers.

She shook her head.

His laugh was husky, uneven, and somehow, despite her lack of experience, she knew he was as surprised by the strength of their desire as she was.

His kiss was slow and explorative at first, but that wasn't enough. This time, it was India who deepened it, hungrily demanding more of him than he was giving her, her body cleaving to his as the car moved through Manhattan. She groaned, the kiss nowhere near enough to satisfy

her, so she moved swiftly, unclicking her seat belt
and pushing up, her dress lifting over her thighs
as she straddled him, rolling her hips in a silent,
eager invitation to his masculine strength. His
arousal was firm between her legs, with far too
much fabric blocking him from her, so a wild
kind of desperation overtook her. As she kissed
him, her fingers moved, thrusting his belt apart,
then his zip, needing more than she could put into
rational thought and words to feel him inside her.

'Please, Khalil,' she said, because she knew
how it drove him wild to hear his name on her
lips. She rolled her hips again, kissing him more,
and then, she lifted her dress over her head, needing to be naked. There was flame burning within
her, a flame he'd lit, and she needed him to control it, to feed it, to eventually extinguish it—but
not for a long time, yet.

He swore at her nakedness, and then his hands
were cupping her breasts, his fingers plucking at
her nipples until she saw stars. Her back arched
and she cried out as he moved one hand between
her legs, brushing against her sex almost by accident as he reached into his pants and freed his
arousal from the confines of his clothing.

She kissed him hard then, lifting up on her
haunches so his hands could dispose of her underpants, pushing them low enough for her to
kick them off. It was instincts that were driving

her, not experience. India had barely any of that, certainly nothing that would guide her in the way of men and pleasure, and yet she moved back to his lap and welcomed him, taking his length deep on a long, slow breath, pleasure exploding as he filled her completely, her muscles stretching to accommodate his generous size.

It was impossible to be aware of the lights that were streaking past their window, the city a shimmering blur in the distance as he rocked his hips and India thrust down on his length, pushing them towards an inevitable, almost immediate climax, tipping her over the edge at the same time he exploded, drawing her close to him, kissing her hard as their bodies united in rapture and joy, their mutual release punctuated by India's frantic cries.

Afterwards, only the sound of their breathing was audible in the back of the car—no sounds of New York permeated the vehicle's bulletproof steel. Even if it had, India wouldn't have heard it. Her ears were full of the rushing of her blood and the exhalation of her breath, her heart turning over at the suddenness—and rightness—of this.

'That was—' She searched for the right word, but Khalil beat her to it.

'Just the beginning.'

Her eyes flared and she smiled, lazy, warm pleasure spreading through her completely. She didn't move; not at first. She didn't want to be parted from him. It was far nicer to feel their bodies melded together, to experience his breath through her chest, to be able to kiss him as she wanted, as the car snaked through the city. But eventually, Khalil ran his fingers lightly over her back, his voice husky. 'We're here.'

She lifted her head to see they were in an underground parking garage.

'Allow me.' As she wriggled off his lap, Khalil retrieved her dress, lifting it over her head then letting it cascade down her body. 'I am already looking forward to removing that all over again.'

Anticipation squeezed all of her organs, so India could barely breathe.

Khalil watched her sleep as the dawn light filtered across Manhattan, resisting a selfish urge to wake her with a kiss. She was exhausted, and with good reason. He'd made love to her for hours, sensually exploring her body with his mouth, his hands, before taking possession of her once more, this time with him calling the shots, drawing her to the brink of orgasm before pulling back, then pushing her close again and again, almost tormenting her with his mastery of her body. All for a good cause, though—her eventual release, when he moved with the intention of gifting it, caused her to cry out so loudly he paused for a moment to ensure she was okay.

His ego was still riding high. They'd swum together in the infinity pool, before making love again, wet and tangled together on the terrace floor, then lain beneath the sky, talking until her eyes grew heavy and she'd fallen asleep, her head heavy on his chest. He'd carried her here rather than disturb her, and still she slept, her face angelic, her body far too beautiful to belong to a mere mortal.

Their night together had exceeded all of his expectations. His libido was impressive, his stamina renowned, and he'd never known a woman to be such a match for him. Her excitement was a thing of perfection; he wanted more of her. It was the first thought that occurred to him, and he grappled with it, frowning. More?

He didn't do more.

One night was all he took from a woman, all he gave of himself. Fatima had made sure of that. His ex-fiancée had ensured he'd never again allow his heart to believe it was anything so foolish as 'in love'. One night was easy. Sex was simple. Chemistry determined the trajectory, the terms were clear, as though spelled out in black and white. Physical pleasure, no promises, no line-crossing, just sex.

But with India, the sex had been enough to lure

him to want more. His mind told him it wasn't possible even as his body was taking control, trying to discover a way that he could enjoy more of her company without risking any emotional complications. His own heart was safe—it had been turned to stone by Fatima's actions—but India wasn't like him. There was a gentleness to her that reminded him, strangely, of Astrid, so that he wanted to protect her even as his body yearned for more.

He left the room before he could weaken, pressing a pod into the coffee machine and watching as golden liquid poured into his cup. He always drank it black and strong, a shot of energy to give mental clarity and to remind Khalil that he could achieve anything.

He carried the cup towards the balcony, his eyes landing on the hotel they'd been at the night before, just able, at this distance, to make out the hint of the balcony they'd moved onto, when he'd wanted to be sure they were alone. Remembering the way they'd kissed then, as though there were a ticking time bomb and only their intimacy could avert its explosion, brought a smile to his face and a hardness to his cock. He sipped the coffee, relishing the bitterness and warmth, the immediate buzz firing through his brain.

A noise sounded across the room and he looked over his shoulder, half expecting to see

India. Only it was his phone, in the kitchen, buzzing. Frowning, he strode towards it, an immediate wave of disgust forming in his belly when he saw Ethan's name on the screen. Last night had started out as a revenge plan, but it had very quickly morphed into something else. He no longer saw India as a means to an end; had he ever?

'What do you want?' he demanded in his most scathing tone—the kind of tone that would ordinarily turn his enemies into jabbering messes.

'Oh, nothing. Just to see how your night went.'

Khalil's brows lifted heavenwards. 'Do you really want to know?'

'Sure. Why not?'

But Khalil shied away from sharing any details—even when he knew they'd drive the other man crazy. He was already regretting the implication he'd made, all for vengeance—India had deserved better. 'I'm sure you can imagine.'

'Yes, you're right about that. I suppose you spent the night together?'

Khalil's hand formed a fist again. He hated this guy with all his heart.

'It's none of your business.'

'Business is an interesting choice of words.' Ethan didn't sound remotely concerned. If anything, he was happy…? Something wasn't adding up.

'What are you getting at, Graves? Spit it out or get the hell off the phone.'

'I presume you know she's a prostitute?'

Khalil was not often blindsided, but the other man's words hit him with all the strength of a knockout punch. He could hear Ethan's smug smile, the delight he had in saying the vulgar lie.

'An expensive one, obviously, or I wouldn't have hired her. But she's very, very good at her job, don't you think?'

It couldn't be true. Nothing about what Ethan was saying tallied with the woman he'd spent the night with. He didn't believe it. This was just Ethan's way of getting his own revenge.

'You are a disgusting excuse for a human being,' Khalil ground out.

Ethan laughed, a cackle that set Khalil's blood raging.

'Her name is India McCarthy, and she works for Warm Engagements Escort Agency. Search online and you'll see her profile.'

Khalil was holding the phone in a fist. He couldn't speak.

'And don't be put off by the wording that says "no sex". I've booked loads of their girls before, using darling Astrid's money, of course, and they're always more than happy to put out— for a small extra fee. I hope you're tipping her as well as I'd planned to, Khalil.' He laughed as he disconnected the call.

Khalil stared at the phone, knowing he'd regret it even as he loaded up an Internet browser and typed in the name Ethan had given him. He was doing it to prove Ethan wrong, not because he believed that bastard.

Her face appeared as soon as he hit 'search'.

Nausea rode through him. It was obvious that Ethan had played Khalil at his own game—and won. Not only had he brought a prostitute home, he'd kissed her at the bar, in full view of Manhattan's social elite, an army of spies armed with cell phones, who would be all too happy to sell this picture to the tabloids. It was Fatima all over again. Fatima's lies, Fatima's trickery, Fatima's mercenary ability to wrap men around her little finger purely for financial gain, her cold-hearted devotion to money the only thing she cared about. And India was just the same! But she wasn't. Was she?

He ran his mind over the night, trying to connect the dots of Ethan's words to the woman he'd bedded. Surely that passion hadn't been faked? No, their chemistry was genuine, of that he was sure, but that didn't mean she wouldn't be willing to exploit it. He'd told her he was royal almost as soon as they'd met. He had no way of knowing if her interest from that point on had been genuine or motivated by his endless coffers, as Fatima's actions had been. But her relationship with Ethan suddenly made so much more sense. It wasn't a relationship. She was too smart for him, too beautiful. She was being paid to be at his side, to laugh at his jokes, to fetch his damned drinks. It was why she'd hesitated to leave Ethan, her current pay cheque, why she'd questioned the fact he only wanted one night with her. If she was going to give up Ethan, it had to be worth it. Everything suddenly made so much sense! It was why she'd wanted to let Ethan down gently, to feign illness, rather than being honest with him. She wanted to have her cake and eat it too! Had she thought she could sleep with Khalil one night and Ethan the next? Disgust chipped at his gut.

He slammed his palms into the kitchen counter, staring at it with a rising sense of outrage. After Fatima, he'd thought he'd protected himself against women like this! He'd thought he could spot them a mile off! How had India managed to get under his skin so thoroughly?

Was there any chance this wasn't true? Was there any possibility? He groaned at his gullibility. What kind of escort agency offered dates with no sex? Not any that he'd ever heard of! Admittedly he had very little experience with such matters, but he was sure a happy ending was a guaranteed part of the night.

With every minute that passed, he began to see India as the second coming of Fatima, to see her as a very beautiful, manipulative, dishonest, scheming woman. Old pain was exposed, bitter and fierce. He stared at her photograph on the phone; the confirmation of her vocation stared right back at him. Damn it! How had he been so foolish?

He put down his phone and straightened his spine, renewed determination firing in his veins. He'd made a mistake, but at least there were no lasting consequences this time. He would wait until she was awake and then he'd throw her out of this apartment, and out of his life. He never wanted to see her again.

'So what exactly is the going rate?'

She frowned, still sleepy, her body on fire, her nerves sensitive, her stomach hungry and mouth dry, and, most of all, her heart blessedly, completely content in a way she'd never known before. Khalil stood in the hotel kitchen, dressed in an expensive bespoke suit that fitted him as though it were moulded to his frame. Naked he was glorious, but like this he was the embodiment of power and success, so a thousand and one sparks went off beneath her skin. Given his formal state of dress, India was glad she'd paused long enough to wrap a sheet, toga-style, around herself.

'For coffee?' she prompted as the fragrance reached her nostrils. 'I'd pay about a thousand dollars right now.'

He didn't smile. 'I meant, for a night of your... company.'

India stopped walking, frozen to the spot. Her smile dropped to her toes and her blood turned to ice. 'I'm sorry?'

'Oh, apologies are definitely warranted,' he said with a cutting tone to his voice.

'That's not what I—what do you mean?'

'Now I understand why you were trying to move our arrangement to tonight,' he said, throwing back half of his own coffee without shifting his eyes from her face. 'You were already booked last night. I suppose you expect me to compensate you for two nights of business?'

Her eyes swept shut as the true horror of the situation became clear.

'I'm just surprised you didn't negotiate your price and ask for payment before you climbed into my bed. Surely that's better business practice?'

India felt sick. 'Don't,' she snapped, slicing her hand through the air. 'Don't you dare suggest that I slept with you in exchange for—'

'Oh, that's rich,' he interrupted. 'Acting outraged when the whole world can see who and what you do.' He lifted up his phone, showing her Warm Engagements profile picture. She felt the sharp sting of tears at her eyes and in her throat, but refused to give in to that weakness now.

'That's a legitimate escort service,' she insisted, but of course she could see how damning the facts were, on the surface.

'Sure it is,' he said in a way that made it obvious he didn't believe a word she was saying. 'Legitimate prostitution.'

'No,' she ground out. 'You're wrong. It's not that kind of agency. We specialise in dates for out-of-town businesspeople, who need someone on their arm for one night and don't want the complication of a romantic entanglement. That concept is the *only* reason I agreed to work for them. I have *never* slept with a man for money, and it definitely isn't what last night was about.'

'That is not what Ethan said.'

Her jaw dropped. 'Ethan?' She groaned, lifting a hand to her forehead and pacing across the room, towards the kitchen. 'You do know him, don't you?'

'Yes.'

'But what did he say? How did he—? He didn't know about you. And us. I mean, he didn't know I left with you.'

'I made sure he did, actually.' Khalil glared

down his nose at her. 'It turns out, you weren't the only one telling lies last night, *azeezi*.' Now when he used the term of endearment she flinched, impossibly hurt by the tone of his voice, the obvious accusation.

'You used me,' she whispered, the words sticking in her throat. But it was the truth, of course. What other explanation was there? Was that why he'd pursued her so relentlessly? Overpowering her very minuscule defences, all because he wanted to hurt the other man? Was that all last night had meant to him? 'Why?'

'You use men for money. Is that any better?'

She stormed across to him without thinking, shoving his chest as a primal, animalistic rage overtook her. 'Damn it, I'm not going to stand here and listen to this! I would *never* sleep with a man for money—never. If you think me possible of that, then you're a terrible judge of character.' Anger made the words vibrate and she clung to that emotion rather than allowing sadness to take over.

'Then don't stand here,' he said, quietly, his words cutting her like glass. 'Our *business* is concluded. Please leave.'

She bit down on her lip, his scathing dismissal undoing a part of her soul. She stared at him, trying to find a trace of the man she'd spent the night with—and failing. He was cold, completely unfamiliar. Part of her wanted to run out of the room immediately and never think of this night again, but at the same time she couldn't live with him believing what he did of her! She'd only slept with one other man—her boyfriend at the time. She was just about as far from being a call girl as it was possible to get.

'I work for an escort agency, yes, but the work is strictly professional. Events like last night, that begin with the client meeting me in the lobby and end in the same way.'

His eyes flashed with contempt. 'Unfortunately, I know Ethan better than that. I have no doubt that if we had not met, you would have spent the night with him instead of me.'

'You're wrong,' she said, numb. 'Being with you was a spontaneous, out-of-character thing for me. I don't go home with men I've just met. I don't make love to people I barely know.'

'And yet you were so very comfortable with it.'

Because you were different, she wanted to scream at him.

'The innocent act worked last night, but I know better now,' he pointed out with quiet, stupid logic. 'All I can hope is that no one managed to catch that ill-conceived kiss at the bar on their cell phone. If it were to go viral that I took a woman like you home, it would be the death of my father.'

'Then it's just as well I have every intention of forgetting this whole night ever happened.'

His lips were a grim line. 'As do I, believe me.'

The dress she'd worn was discarded on the floor. She scooped it up and pulled it on quickly, scanning for her shoes and handbag—which were blessedly near the front door. She slid her feet into the heels, swallowing back a sob, and thrust her handbag under her arm. She didn't even turn around and look at him; she couldn't. Her mind was all over the place, her pride in tatters. She waited until the door had slammed shut behind her before breaking into a run, sprinting the length of the hallway and pressing the button for the lift. India desperately wanted to put the whole sordid ordeal behind her, but even as she swore to herself she'd do exactly that, she felt terrified of how difficult it would be. Last night hadn't been an ordinary event—it was the kind of night that imprinted on a person's soul, and she knew, even as she desperately pushed him from her mind, that she would never forget Sheikh Khalil el Abdul.

He watched her leave with a sinking feeling in the pit of his stomach. He was so angry with her! So angry with Ethan! So angry with the world, if he were honest. But he was especially angry with India, because she'd made him forget every promise he'd made himself after Fatima. When he was with India, he'd felt as if the world was good again, he'd felt as if he could smile, for the first time in years. He'd enjoyed himself, and his grief and loss had been so far away.

Discovering it was all part of her job description chipped away at an essential part of him, so he didn't—couldn't—stop to think if there was even a chance he was wrong.

Would he have felt so vehemently if not for Fatima? Would his rage have been so quick to spark? Or might he have given her more of a chance to explain herself? He couldn't say, but with every minute that passed in the wake of her departure, he felt a mix of shame and disappointment, frustration clipping through him.

Ethan had thrown her identity in his face, and the other man had his own reasons for wanting to hurt Khalil. But what about the website? What about the fact she did in fact work for an escort agency? Was there any chance she was telling the truth?

He ground his teeth together, throwing his head back and staring at the ceiling.

And what did it matter? Even before he knew this, they'd agreed it would simply be one night.

His life was in Khatrain, and it was time for him to get on with it. He simply had to forget India McCarthy ever existed.

CHAPTER FOUR

'OH, GOD, NO.' She stared at the pregnancy test with a sinking feeling in the pit of her stomach, her worst nightmares confirmed. Six weeks after rushing from the penthouse apartment she'd shared with Khalil, India finally had an explanation for all the strange symptoms she'd been experiencing. The exhaustion, nausea, sore back and rioting emotions had been easy to explain on their own, but her skipped menstrual cycle was the final straw. It was only when writing overdue bills in her calendar that suspicion had formed.

It couldn't be true. Surely fate wouldn't be so desperately miserable as to throw this complication into her already careening out of control life? She looked around the home desperately, as the future seemed to twist away from her completely.

'Pregnant?' She groaned, shaking her head and laughing at the same time—this couldn't be true!

The realisation hit her that she was alone. No, she corrected herself. She'd have Jackson, and, even though their finances were in a parlous state, somehow, she'd cope. Her parents would expect that of her, and for them, she'd do this.

On autopilot, she strode into the kitchen and opened the top drawer, where she'd stashed the envelope, the morning after returning from Khalil's hotel room. He must have put it in her bag while she slept; she hadn't discovered it until she'd returned home. She'd been too numb to do more than reach for her bus pass at first, but then, she'd needed her keys and that had required a more detailed rifle through her bag. It was only then that she'd identified the envelope with thick black lettering on the front.

You earned this.

Her heart had thudded to a stop as she'd opened the envelope to discover a cheque—grey in colour with gold lettering and the intricate emblem of the Khatrain royal family. The cheque was made out to her, for an absurd amount, more than she earned in a month—or had earned, before losing her job.

'*This is a reputable agency, India. I will not have the name of this business dragged into disrepute by young women who are looking for an extra way to earn income. You will no longer be*

listed on our books. There are several other...
businesses...that deal in the kind of work you do.'

She had been mortified and offended, and then terrified. Keeping her younger brother Jackson at college was all her responsibility, and on top of attempting to maintain her parents' mortgage, so that she didn't lose their family home, India already struggled to make ends meet. Without the booking fees from Warm Engagements, she had no hope.

Why hadn't she cashed the cheque sooner? Because she *hadn't* earned it. And to cash it would be some sort of tacit acceptance of his accusations. Now, though, the cheque took on a new meaning, as she imagined all of the expenses involved in carrying out a pregnancy and then delivering a baby. Courtesy of her mother's cancer treatments, India was no stranger to hospitals and what they charged—there were some bills still outstanding. There were also the baby's needs once it was born. She could thrift shop a lot of things, but certain items would have to be purchased new, and there would be a period of time when she was unable to work altogether. What would she do for childcare? There was no one who could help her.

How was she going to do this, and all on her own?

But she *had* to. For the sake of their baby, she

had to find a way to manage. And the cheque Khalil had written was a good place to start. To hell with her pride; there was a baby to consider.

Khalil had truly hoped she wouldn't cash the damned thing. He didn't realise how much he'd needed that assurance until his bank in New York called to advise him that the cheque had been brought in that morning. It was all the confirmation he needed— not that it had been necessary. A cursory investigation by his security team had shown that she was a popular employee of the agency, going on multiple dates a week. They'd been unable to confirm her assertion about meeting men at the events, however society photographs had captured more than enough images of India being held tight by her dates, the intimate nature of the pictures making it impossible to believe that things were as innocent as she claimed.

Why had she waited six weeks to cash the cheque? It was a question that barely mattered. She'd lived up to what he'd thought of her, it was time to stop remembering the night they'd shared. It had been the worst mistake of his life; he could only be grateful his father had been spared the mortification of tabloid speculation about it. Their kiss had not gone public.

It was not appropriate that he continued to think of her, that she played such a part in his fantasies night after night. Somehow, her betrayal stung almost as much as Fatima's. When he looked back, there was a part of him that had, on some level, always known Fatima for what she was: mercenary and opportunistic. He'd fallen in love with her quick wit and fun-loving attitude, but there had been something in her eyes that had been appraising, always, something that had held parts of him back from her as well. But with India, he'd been completely fooled, her innocent act so easy to buy into.

He scraped back his chair, pacing towards the windows that overlooked the capital city of Takistan and, in the distance, the Persian Gulf—which, today, sparkled as though a net of diamonds had been cast over its surface.

At twenty-nine years of age, he knew he could delay no longer: his country required him to marry before his thirtieth birthday, when he would become King of Khatrain. It was necessary to choose a suitable bride—he could no longer think about India. She didn't deserve it.

Only his mind was not obeying him today, and India continued to flash before his eyes, as she'd been in the car on the way back to his suite. She was an excellent actress, he'd give her that. His lips twisted in a mocking smile as he reached for his phone.

'Have my horse readied. I intend to ride west.'

He gripped the receiver more tightly. 'I do not know,' he responded to the question of, 'for how long?' and then disconnected the call. The desert was an essential part of his soul, and it was there that he could clear his mind of the American call girl—an obvious mistake—once and for all.

'He is still unavailable, madam.' India stood like a flamingo in the kitchen, one foot propped against her opposite knee, her hand resting on the bench to her left. The other pressed to her still-flat stomach as she tilted her head to catch the phone between her ear and shoulder. It was a warm day and pregnancy hormones—in full flight despite the fact she was only eight weeks along—were making her tired, nauseous, anxious and cranky. She had been attempting to contact Khalil for over a week, ever since she'd decided he deserved the courtesy of the information at least.

Only contacting a royal was no mean feat.

'Well, when will he be available?' she snapped, although it wasn't this low-level staff member's fault that Khalil had disappeared into thin air.

'I cannot say, madam. My apologies.' The line went dead.

India made a deranged laughing sound as she placed her cell phone on the bench. Was he dodging her calls? Or truly unavailable? She suspected the former, and it made her furious to think that he wouldn't even give her the courtesy of a conversation after that night. But then, she'd seen his anger when he'd accused her of being a prostitute. She'd left his hotel with no question in her mind that he hated her—and truly wished to never see her again.

'Well, tough,' she said softly, patting her stomach. 'I know what it's like to be abandoned by your dad and I'm not going to let that happen to you, little one. At least, not without a fight.'

She knew a little about Khatrain—bits and pieces garnered through her life, and studies—but most of her knowledge related to their economy. It was dry, black-and-white information about their oil industry and burgeoning tech sector with their headquarters in the then fledgling city of Takistan. Only Takistan was now a stunning metropolis, a sprawling construction of steel and glass that burst from the earth. The dusk sky gave it a perfect backdrop, the gradient colours spreading from purple to gold and orange highlighting the twinkling lights of the monoliths in the foreground. She craned her neck to see the city better, admiring not just its modernity but also its proximity to the ocean, which curved around it like a ribbon, and had been diverted, at some point, to create several canals that ran as veins between the buildings.

'Beautiful,' she said with a shake of her head, earning an approving nod from the man beside her. Their elbows had been engaged in a silent battle for the duration of the flight, the too-small seats and narrow armrest far from ideal for the number of hours she'd had to spend cramped between her neighbour and the portal window. But it had all been worth it to secure this exceptional vantage point of the city as they descended.

The plane was climate-controlled. It was only once the doors were opened that a rush of hot air blasted into the cabin and India had to brace herself against the seat in front. Nausea rose in her chest. She grabbed a mint from her purse and sucked on it—this was the only thing she'd been able to discover that helped with the waves of sickness that assaulted her occasionally.

Their aircraft had been towed to a distant terminal—the budget airlines' designated space—and there was no air-conditioned aerobridge leading inside. Instead, there were stairs, wheeled to the doors of the plane, and a large, sweeping route around another aeroplane before they were ushered through security doors and passport control.

India stifled several yawns as she shuffled along the queue, grateful when at last she was beckoned forward.

'And the purpose for your visit?' the woman, stunning with her dark eyes and lips that had been painted a deep red, murmured as she scanned the passport.

To tell your bastard of a sheikh he's going to be a father then get the heck out of Dodge, she imagined saying, a tight smile curving her lips. 'To see an old friend.'

'Social.' The woman nodded, ticking a box. 'How long do you intend to stay?'

'Twenty-four hours.' And though it wasn't necessary, she flashed the printout of her return ticket, her escape route already planned. She would do whatever she could to give the Sheikh this information, and then she would leave. If he still refused to see her, then at least she could tell their baby that she'd tried. She knew first-hand the importance of that. And if he refused to let her leave? The idea flashed into her mind suddenly, so she froze, her eyes wide, before she discounted it. He'd be as glad to see the back of her as last time.

'Such a short visit. It is a shame. There is much in Khatrain to see—many wonders to enjoy.'

'I'm sure there are. Unfortunately, I have commitments back home.'

The woman reached for a stamp, clicked it onto India's passport, then slid it across. 'Enjoy your brief trip, then, madam.'

Again, India was buffeted by the heat when she stepped out of the airport, so she lifted a hand to her face, waving it rhythmically. There was a long queue for taxis, and she waited with depleting energy. Her plan had been to go to her hotel first and freshen up, before attempting to contact Khalil, but now that she was here, she simply wanted to get this over with.

When she finally slipped into a taxi—with at least some air conditioning—it cooled her rising temperature. She stared at the hotel's information, opened her mouth and then closed it again. 'The royal palace, please.'

The driver met her eyes in the mirror and India was grateful she had over a year's experience attending glittering social events in Manhattan. If she'd learned anything, it was how to act as though she belonged anywhere. 'Is there a problem?' Her tone was stiff, her demeanour imposing.

'Of course not, madam. Right away.'

The car pulled into traffic and India allowed her head to drop backwards, against the leather seat of the car. For a moment, she closed her eyes, needing to restore a little of her energy.

Only Khalil was there, as always, his face haunting her, so there was no real respite. She woke with sweat beading her brow, just as the car drew to a stop.

'This is as close as I can get,' the driver said, gesturing to the large golden gates in the foreground of, without a doubt, the largest and most magnificent building India had ever seen—whether in real life or photographs. Her jaw dropped and the magnitude of what she was about to do sent a tremble down her spine.

Her baby was a part of all this. And she'd had no idea just quite what that entailed—she had been imagining Khalil and Khalil alone, without quite realising what his title meant. He was going to be King, and their child would be—what? His heir? Or an embarrassment? Was she making things worse by coming here? What if he refused to acknowledge their baby? Was it worse if she'd told him and Khalil made that decision? Was it better for the baby to believe its father had never known? Could she do anything to make this better?

But what if he *did* want to know the baby and be a part of his or her life? India had barely known her father—he'd blown into her life when it had suited him, then disappeared for months or years, so she'd never been able to count on him. What if Khalil wanted to be a real part of their child's life, to see him or her regularly, to call and ask how their day went? India would have given her eye teeth for that, and she would fight for the chance for her baby to know that kind of love.

Even though there was a real risk that it could backfire.

'Thank you.' She paid the driver before opening her door. She was prepared for the heat this time, though it still dried her eyes out. She pulled her sunglasses into place and hitched a small backpack over one shoulder, standing and staring at the palace as the taxi driver sped off.

Turrets of white stood high in the sky like puffs of cream atop large round towers. Some were golden, others pale, and there was a large open courtyard lined on all sides by palm trees that cast spiky shadows across the marbled floor. A fountain stood in the very centre, spurting water in several directions, before landing in a large oval-shaped pool. Her mouth went dry at the very visage. She turned her attention to that barrier, scanning it thoughtfully, until her eyes landed on the security guard nearest to her. There were several, standing every ten feet or so, staring out at the road, ever watchful. The man in front of India had his eyes on her, so she smiled—it was not returned. His hands were at his sides, but at his hip he wore a pistol and a large rifle was holstered diagonally across his back. Though his uniform was ceremonial, she had no doubt he had full military training. Fear shifted through her, but India had come this far; she wasn't about to be turned back now.

'Excuse me,' she said, when she reached the man.

He didn't say anything, but his eyes met hers, curiosity in their depths.

'How do I get inside?'

He regarded her with evident surprise. 'Do you have an invitation?'

She thought quickly, playing out multiple scenarios in her head. If she said that she didn't, she would likely be turned away immediately. There was no guarantee that any words she uttered would even make it to Khalil's ears—except for one sentence.

'I do, yes. His Highness Khalil el Abdul sent for me.'

The man's expression changed immediately. He lifted his walkie-talkie—propped on the hip that lacked a gun—and began to speak in his own language, harsh words that she didn't understand.

'Your name?' He switched back to English. Butterflies burst through her.

'India McCarthy.'

He repeated her name into the walkie-talkie.

'Documentation?'

'It was a phone call,' she lied. 'He asked me to come over the phone.'

'Identification documentation,' he clarified.

'Oh.' Heat stained her cheeks as she reached into her bag and lifted out her passport. 'Here.'

She held it up for him but he took it, turning away from her and moving to another guard. That guard left with the passport, and the original returned to his post.

Something like anxiety tightened in her gut. 'Where's he going?'

The original guard didn't answer. She was grateful that the sun was low in the sky, as she stood waiting for a long time—at least twenty minutes. Already fatigued, weary and emotionally exhausted, she wanted to cry, but wouldn't give the guard—or anyone—the satisfaction. Eventually, Original Guard's walkie-talkie began to crackle. A brow shot up, before he gestured about three hundred metres down the fence. 'There is a gate. Go to it; someone will take you from there.'

India nodded her thanks. It was a long walk, and, given the heat, she didn't rush. Eventually, she reached the gate, where several guards were waiting. Anxiety grew.

'This way, please.' A woman gestured without smiling towards the marble courtyard. India followed behind, aware of the two guards who came to flank her. As they passed the fountain she stopped walking, giving into temptation despite the certainty it would earn the disapproval of her companions. She moved to the water and quickly lowered her hands, splashing some onto her forearms and neck, instantly refreshing. The female guard stood waiting, her face impassive. No, not impassive, India realised. There was almost something like sympathy in her beautiful eyes.

'It has been particularly hot this summer,' the guard said, slowing her pace a little.

India could have wept for the small kindness from this random stranger. To be spoken to with something approaching civility was beyond her expectations—and it was badly needed!

'I had prepared for heat, but this caught me unawares.'

'Tourists find it hard to bear at first.'

Whatever reply India had been going to make died on her lips as they swept through a set of double doors—each several metres wide, and at least four times her height. The foyer they were in was clearly a 'nuts and bolts' part of the palace—with security apparatus and a minimum of décor—and yet it was still impossibly grand, with high ceilings, chandeliers, marble floors, and artwork adorning every bare space on the walls, so that her eyes were almost overwhelmed with the visual feast.

'You will need to pass through security,' the

woman said, gesturing to the large scanners, the same as India had passed through at the airport.

'Okay.' She bit down on her lip, placing her bag on the tray so it could be whisked along a conveyor belt, then stepping through the frame. Just as at the airport, the scanner did not register any problems.

'Good.' The woman even smiled, so India's butterflies were somewhat allayed, momentarily. With that hurdle crossed through, there was now the task of telling Khalil he was going to be a father—a conversation she was utterly dreading. If only she could have sent a text or email, but she had no direct way of contacting him.

'Will you take me to Khalil now?'

The woman's expression was startled. 'His Highness Sheikh el Abdul has been informed of your arrival. I am not yet aware of when he will see you. Please, take a seat while you wait.'

India's nerves were on the brink of fraying. *Are you kidding me?* She shook her head as she moved towards the seat the guard had indicated, easing herself into it. She was too wound up to relax, though, far too coiled to enjoy the comfort of the armchair. She fidgeted with her fingers in her lap for the first hour, before frustration got the better of her and she moved towards the man behind the computer screen, who'd scanned her handbag.

'Excuse me, sir, are you able to get an update on the Sheikh's schedule for me?'

The guard looked at her as though she'd asked him to swim to Mars. 'His Highness will see you when he can. If he decides to see you at all.'

If? India hadn't even thought of that. What if, even now, he refused to meet her? Tears sprang to her eyes and she turned around quickly, before the man could see her. Odious, horrible person!

Thirty minutes later and a door opened, so she stood, apprehensively, but it was just a servant wheeling a trolley. She came towards India before stopping, lifting the lid off the top tray.

'Some refreshments, madam.'

India stared at the food and felt instantly sick. She dug her fingernails into her palm, trying to control it, but the waves of nausea were growing stronger. 'Is there a restroom?' she demanded urgently.

The woman nodded and gestured to a purple door. India broke into a run and just made it, heaving over the toilet until her stomach was empty and her hairline moist with perspiration. When she emerged, the servant had gone but the tray remained. India was able to pick over it now, choosing a plain bread roll with some butter, and draining the glass of iced tea far too quickly. She sat down again, frustrated and angry.

Another hour passed. She approached the

guard once more, her mind made up. 'I'd like to leave. Would you help me organise a taxi to the city?'

The guard met her eyes, shrugged, then spoke into his walkie-talkie. She bit down on her lip, the reality of her situation landing squarely between her eyes. She'd wasted money she couldn't afford on flying to Khatrain, all because she'd believed there might be a shred of decency in Khalil. Why had she even thought such a thing after the way he'd spoken to her the last time they'd met? The things he'd said to her, the look of hatred in his eyes—she should have known better than to hope.

She pulled tighter on her handbag strap and waited, her arms crossed. It was only minutes but, given India had already been waiting for several hours, she was ready to burst something when, finally, another door opened. This time, three guards swept through, and behind them, Khalil. But not as he'd been in New York. Then, he'd been spectacular-looking but somehow familiar to her. Now, he was so fascinating and majestic that, even though her heart was flooded with hate, she found that all she could do was stare at him as he stormed towards her. He wore long white robes that breezed behind him with the speed of his stride, and his body was broad and powerful, even more so dressed like this. His eyes bored into hers and she felt the same rush of anger she'd known on that last morning, the hatred and disrespect. Her heart flip-flopped. 'Khalil,' she said as he drew close, and one guard gasped.

'Your Highness,' he corrected coldly, without breaking his pace. 'Follow me.'

The lack of courtesy was surprising even after all that had passed between them. None-theless, she had come here with one thing in mind, and she intended to carry out her objective. She scooped up her bag and fell into step behind him, but she had to half run to keep up. He moved away from this pragmatic entrance-way and into a corridor—though, really, it was as wide as at least four corridors, and decorated with ancient-looking furniture on both sides, including enormous vases of flowers that were totally un-familiar to her, exotic and spiky, like something out of a fairy tale. Their fragrance was sweet, and, in her current state, India's nausea returned with a vengeance.

'Will you slow down a bit?' she asked, slow-ing her own pace accordingly, pressing a hand to her hip.

Khalil stopped walking and turned to look at her, exasperated. But as his eyes scanned her face there was, for a moment, something like concern. Perhaps there was a hint of humanity in the man after all?

'You are ill?'

'Well.' She put her other hand on her hip, glaring at him with undisguised irritation. 'Let's see, shall we? I've endured a cramped plane trip, a hot taxi ride, a stand-off out the front of your palace with an armed guard who was clearly hostile, and then hours in a room waiting for Your Royal Highness to decide to see me. How do you think I feel?'

If India had been less angry, she might have noticed the blanching of the guards' faces at her tirade to their Prince, but she was in her own bubble, completely incapable of thinking clearly or acting calmly.

Khalil was used to his guards and didn't mind their presence in any respect. He paced towards her, his eyes sparking with hers. 'You arrive unannounced and expect what, India? That I might roll out the red carpet? And what exactly in our interaction gave you any idea I would be glad to see you again?' He leaned closer, lowering his voice. 'We agreed we would both forget what happened.'

She looked away, wondering if he'd been able to do that so easily. For India, Khalil had been burned into her mind, so she saw him all the time, dreamed of him, woke up reaching for him…

'Believe me, I don't particularly relish being here, but you gave me little choice. Had you accepted any of my attempts to contact you, then we could have dealt with this over the phone. You left with me no choice.'

'On the contrary, I left you with a very clear choice—to stay out of my life.'

Her lips parted and now she saw the guards, their faces carefully blanked of emotion, and embarrassment swept through her. 'Is there somewhere more private we can speak? I just need a few moments of your time, Your Highness.' She imbued his title with as much scathing cynicism as she could, easily matching a tone he had employed in the past when speaking to her.

'I was taking us somewhere more private when you demanded that we stop.'

She compressed her lips. 'I asked you to slow down; that's not the same thing.'

It was obvious that Khalil was not used to being contradicted—and she enjoyed that fact. He deserved nothing better than to be strenuously put in his place. If it weren't for the conversation that was to follow, she could almost have enjoyed the awkwardness of their interaction. But this was just the prelude to what would necessarily follow, and India could see quite clearly that it was not going to be as simple as informing him of her pregnancy. She'd run straight into the lion's den and she would need to think fast to get out alive.

CHAPTER FIVE

'So?'

Her stomach was in a constant cycle of loop-the-loops. She wasn't sure if it was deliberate or not, but the room he'd led her to was impossibly intimidating. Vaulted ceilings with a wall made of glass on one side, framing a view of the city that now, given the lateness of the hour, twinkled against the black of the sky. The floor in here was mosaic and very old, and at the front of the room there were two large thrones, gold and marble, imposing and grand. The flower arrangements in the corridor had given way to enormous trees in golden pots, some wrapping tendrils around the marble pillars that stretched like limbs towards the ceiling. His voice echoed in the room and she shivered, an unintentional response to the emotions of that moment.

'You have come to my palace and demanded to see me, yet now stand mute. Are you here simply to waste my time?'

Outrage fired through her, finally slotting her brain into gear. 'I just hadn't expected your palace to be quite so…palatial,' she finished lamely, crossing her arms over her chest, then regretting the gesture when his eyes dropped to the hint of cleavage exposed by her simple white linen blouse. She wore it tucked into her faded jeans, with cream sliders that revealed pale pink toenails. It was a simple, elegant outfit but under his inspection she felt as though she were wearing lingerie. Desire stirred in her stomach, catching her completely off guard. How could she feel *anything* but revulsion for this man?

'Why don't we cut to the chase?' he murmured. 'Tell me how much you want.'

She frowned, not understanding.

'You cashed the cheque I gave you; I presume you want more? Is it blackmail, India? Are you demanding money in exchange for your silence?'

Heat fired behind her eyes. 'How dare you?'

His smile was cynical. 'I'm sure you can understand why I think you capable of this.'

'No, actually,' she muttered. 'I have wracked my brain for anything that happened between us that night that would justify your harsh opinion of me, and drawn a blank. At no point did I say or do anything to give you the impression I sleep with men for payment. That you would think me capable of that says more about you than it does me.'

For a moment his eyes flashed with uncertainty, but it was gone again almost immediately, harsh contempt usurping it. 'We have already discussed the matter of your employment. Frankly, it's none of my business. You can do what you want with your life, but do not involve me again.'

'And that's it? Case closed?'

'There is no case. I have no interest in debating this matter with you. If you need more money, tell me how much and I will have my aid cut you a cheque.'

Her lips parted in surprise. Of course such a thing would be easy for him, but it still made her head spin to imagine the ease with which he was making that offer. After all, India had spent the morning looking under the sofa cushions for loose change, to be sure she could cover her bus fare to the airport.

Take the money and run! Get out while you still can... 'Are you so afraid of people finding out you slept with me that you would effectively offer me a blank cheque?'

'I would prefer to keep news of our liaison private, yes.' His lips compressed and India felt there was more he wasn't saying, something serious and sombre. 'It would be far from ideal to have this story breaking in the press right as I am due to announce my engagement.'

'Your engagement?' She froze to the spot, her eyes scanning his face. She'd thought he couldn't hurt her more than he already had, but those simple words pulled at something deep in her soul, so she spun around, looking for support—and found none. Her knees were trembling, almost unequal to the task of supporting her. He was engaged? Had he been engaged that night? She hated to think she'd been so wrong about him…

'I am to marry before my thirtieth birthday. It is required in order to assure my ascendence to the throne.'

'I see,' she mumbled, numb, moving towards the windows purely so she could prop her hip against something steady.

Your father has remarried, darling. He won't be able to make it to your party after all.'

Soon Khalil would be married, and shortly after that he would have children of his own, children who were his true heirs, children he would actually want. Her brow broke out in hot and cold, memories of her own childhood horribly close, the feeling of rejection that had surrounded her again and again as she'd grappled with the fact her father had made a very deliberate choice not to know nor love her. Was history going to repeat itself?

'So you might understand why I would offer any amount of money to ensure your continued cooperation. Name your price, and I will willingly pay it.'

Oh, how tempting it was! She could simply state an amount—an exorbitant amount that would see Jackson through college and clear all her mother's medical debts, an amount that would mean she could stay home with their baby for the first year of his or her life, with no worries or stress, and then afford childcare afterwards when she was ready to return to work. Heck, she could ask him for enough to cover her own college fees and she could finish her beloved economics degree, and get the kind of job she'd known she wanted ever since she was a schoolgirl!

And what would she tell their baby? Oh, it wouldn't matter for years, but one day the baby would be a child and then an adolescent, and they would look into her eyes and ask her about their dad—would she ever be able to meet their questions if she'd lied to Khalil, and prevented him from having a part in their child's future?

Panic spread through her, because she knew she could accept his money and walk out—not exactly with her head held high but with her needs met, at least—and yet she would never take that option. It was the coward's way, and if her epic journey here today had proven anything, it was that India was no coward.

'Thank you for your offer, but that is not why I'm here.'

He was silent, and she kept her gaze averted, her eyes focussed on the distant city, its shimmering lights offering solace and reminding her of Manhattan. She tried not to think about the view from the balcony, when he'd led her outside and kissed her as though he were drowning and she his sole lifeline.

'Perhaps you could get to the point, then. I do not have all night to stand here with you.'

She turned slowly, keeping her back pressed to the glass. He spoke as though he had plans, and perhaps he did. Maybe he'd been with another woman, making love to her, driving her as wild as he'd driven India. Jealousy spiked through her and she dug her fingernails into her palms to control her heated flashbacks.

'It is a shame that you believed Ethan,' she said quietly, her voice softened by hate. 'I don't know why he lied to you, but he did. I'm not what he accused me of. I'm not what you think.'

Impatience sparked in his gaze, but his voice rang with cool control. 'Why does it matter? That night was a mistake—not the first of my life, but one I have learned from. If I could undo it, I would. As for your request for money, it could have been made from America; there was no need to arrive at my palace gates so dramatically.'

Her jaw dropped at the unfairness of that. 'I beg your pardon, Khalil, but I *tried* to speak to you over the phone and you were always "unavailable". If there had been any other choice, I would have avoided coming here, I promise.'

'I don't believe you.'

'What a surprise.'

His eyes narrowed. 'If your goal is to blackmail me, then arriving like this, inspiring gossip and interest from my palace staff, would only serve to provide me with the necessary motivation to silence you.'

'Then it's just as well blackmail isn't the point of my trip.'

'Then what is?'

She ground her teeth together, sadness washing over her. It had been a single night in a lifetime of nights, and yet, for all their time together was brief, she had felt an undeniable connection to this man. Beyond a connection, she'd felt a sameness, an understanding, as though in some vital way they had been forged from the same elements.

She'd been wrong.

'Come on, India. Name the amount you want so we can both move on.'

She thrust her hands onto her hips and straightened off the glass, but without its support she was instantly woozy, swooning a little before she caught herself. He moved quickly, instincts no doubt firing to life because if he'd paused to consider his actions, he might have chosen to stay where he was and let her drop to the cold hard floor. But instead, he crossed to her quickly, catching her behind her back, holding her to him. From a distance he'd seemed so cold and in command, but like this, she felt it—his warmth and fire, the harsh ructions within his chest as he controlled his breathing, his anger, and something more, barely contained within him. All she could do was look up into his eyes, desire storming through her, the night they'd shared a memory that was so fresh for India she almost felt as though they were travelling back in time.

Kiss me. The idea flared in her mind and terrified her. India pulled away, still unsteady, but needing space before she did something stupid and actually *begged* him to kiss her for real.

'I'm fine,' she lied as exhaustion and nausea threatened to swallow her. 'I just want to get this over with.'

'On this, we are in agreement.'

'I have a flight booked for tomorrow afternoon, and accommodation arranged at a hotel in the city. As soon as we have had this…conversation… I will leave this palace, and shortly thereafter your country, with no intention of coming back. I am not here to threaten you, nor to blackmail you. I am not here to ask you for money—at least, not directly.' He lifted a single, mocking brow. 'I came because I needed to tell you something about that night.'

India was at a crossroads, on the brink of moving in a direction from which she could never return. Once she'd told him about the baby, there was no going back: he would know that he would be a father, regardless of what he chose to do with that information.

'I'm listening.'

'I know.' That was part of the problem. He was staring at her as though he could pull her apart, piece by piece, and examine her until he was satisfied. Anxiety pulsed in her veins.

'I'm not asking you for anything, nor am I expecting anything of you. I'm telling you this because I—well, for personal reasons—feel it's very important that you should have all the information.'

'I have never known anyone to prevaricate to this degree.'

She looked across the room and her gaze inadvertently landed on the thrones. Thrones that belonged to his parents and would soon pass to

Khalil and his wife, and then to their children. Biting back a small sob, she pressed her hand over her stomach, sympathy for the little person who would surely grow up being unwanted and unacknowledged by their father landing in her gut like a rock. It was a pain she knew far too well.

'I'm getting to it.' Her tongue darted out, licking her dry, lower lip, and while her gaze continued to rest on the thrones, his eyes were squarely on her face, following the movement of her tongue as though he couldn't look away.

'The thing is, Khalil, there's no easy way to tell you this,' she whispered, her voice almost lost in the cavernous room. 'I'm pregnant.'

The dropping of a pin would have been easily audible. He said nothing for so long that she wrenched her eyes back to his face, trying to read how he might be feeling. Except it wasn't possible. There was a look of steel in his eyes, his features set in a mask of cold rejection.

'And?'

She frowned, her heart plummeting. 'And, I thought you should know. I—didn't see a lot of my birth father growing up. I wish… I just thought…' but this was going to be a case of history repeating itself. He was clearly showing no intention of acknowledging their baby.

'I just thought you should know,' she finished

weakly, unable to believe he would be so callous in the wake of her news. 'And now, I'd like to go to my hotel, please.'

He stood more still than the marble columns that ran through the room, his body held tight with a tension radiating from his gut to his brain. Her words were detonating inside him, tiny little bombs, going off again and again. She was watching him, waiting for him to speak, and yet he didn't trust himself to say anything just yet.

'Goodbye, Khalil.' Her features crumpled in her beautiful face—how could he still find her so stunning after what she'd proven herself capable of? What he knew her to be? She was every bit as bad as Fatima, exploiting her power with men for financial gain. That should make him despise her on every level, but when he'd held her a moment ago, he'd been so tempted to kiss her, to claim her just as he had that night. What the hell was wrong with him?

He watched her slow movements towards the door—she seemed fatigued and ill and, despite what had happened between them, he found it impossible to ignore her obvious suffering. Clenching his hands into fists at his sides, he moved to catch her, his stride easily doubling hers, so it was only seconds until he was with her.

'Stop.' He spoke with easy command.

She didn't. At no point had she acquiesced to his wishes. Not before she knew who he was, and not now, even when surrounded by this palace and an army of guards.

'India, do not take another step.'

She whirled around to face him then, her face so pale his worry spiked. 'Why not, Khalil? Do you need to insult me a little more for my apparent lifestyle? Or are you going to tell me you need a paternity test before we can discuss this further?'

The reality of her words began to crack through his frozen brain, and for the first time it occurred to him that she was telling the truth. That India was pregnant—and with his baby? Or another man's she was looking to foist on him? Perhaps the paternity test was a wise place to start. 'Could you blame me, given your vocation?'

Her skin paled but she tilted her chin, her gaze defiant even as her lips were trembling. 'I haven't slept with anyone else in a long time, so there's no doubt in my mind that this child is yours. But if you don't believe me, I don't even care any more. I did what I came here to do—I told you about our baby. Now I can go home with a clear conscience.'

He felt hot and cold at once, as Fatima morphed into his mind, the way she'd thrown her abortion at him at the same time as ending their engagement. The baby he'd been unable to protect had been a dagger in his side ever since. There was no way he'd allow this baby to come to any harm. He would die to protect it. Who knew what India would do when she left here?

But he needed to act with care—this was a delicate situation and, despite the fact he could block her from leaving the country, he didn't want to strong-arm her into anything unless it was absolutely necessary, and only because he would do whatever it took to protect this baby.

His expression was grim as he regarded her, his body strong and unyielding even when his heart was thumping into his ribs so hard it was like an anvil. 'This is not the place to have this discussion,' he said, after a moment, looking around the room. He'd brought her to the least comfortable place he could think of, intentionally seeking to inspire awe of his position, but she was clearly not well, and he wasn't so barbaric that he didn't feel a responsibility to protect her—pregnant or not.

'You think?' she snapped, moving away from him. 'I'm not sure there's any place to discuss this that would make a difference, though, to be honest. You've made up your mind about me and nothing I say or do is going to change it. I'm glad I told you, but now you can go back to ignoring me. I don't need anything from you.'

He didn't bother arguing with her—there was no point. He had a pretty clear idea of what her pregnancy would mean for them both, it was simply a matter of working out the finer points of the arrangement. 'You will spend the night here. In the morning, we can speak about this further.'

Her lips parted. 'I will do no such thing. Do you honestly think I would ever go near you again?'

It took him a moment to understand what she'd meant. That he was propositioning her to join him in his bed? 'One night with you was a mistake—and I do not intend to repeat it,' he said firmly, even as desire stirred, tightening his body, making him ache for her. 'I meant for you to sleep in a guest bedroom.'

'I have a hotel room booked,' she demurred, stepping backwards.

'It is too late to be travelling into the city on your own.'

'And whose fault is that?' she demanded with a stamp of her foot. 'I was kept waiting for hours.'

He crossed his arms. 'Let us not lay blame now. The past is irrelevant. We need to focus on the baby, and what is in their best interests.'

She nodded, but her eyes were wary, looking for a trap. 'That's exactly what I think. I despise you after the way you treated me but that doesn't change the fact you're going to be this baby's father. And so long as you can treat him or her with respect and love, then I don't see why you can't be a part of the baby's life, in some way or another.'

He instantly rejected the picture she painted— that he would be the kind of father who flew in and out of his own child's life, a temporary, transient parent that the child never really got to know.

'We can discuss the details in the morning. Come, I will show you to a guest suite.'

In truth, India was so exhausted, she would have much preferred to simply go along with his suggestion, but a warning beacon blared, so she shook her head again. 'I have a hotel room booked. All I need is a ride into the city. We can meet for breakfast and discuss this further. The hotel has a nice restaurant—'

'If we were to meet at a hotel restaurant, everyone would know our business,' he snapped. 'And as you seem unaware of the importance of your pregnancy, allow me to spell it out for you: the baby you claim to be carrying—if true—is the heir to the throne of Khatrain. As such, for the duration of your pregnancy, you are one of the most important people in the kingdom and your security is my responsibility. I will not have you wandering through a hotel lobby in the middle of the night, understood?'

Her lips parted on a rush of breath. 'But…no one knows about us and no one knows about the pregnancy! There is no risk to me.'

'That is a decision I will make.'

'You cannot make decisions about my life with such unilateral authority,' she insisted, and he felt it again, that sharp spurt of desire, like an electric livewire—just the same as the night they'd met, and often since. What was it about this woman that made his body burn?

'Actually, I can,' he said with a shrug, as though it barely mattered to him. 'You are in Khatrain, pregnant with my child. That makes you my responsibility. Furthermore, here my will is absolute, and I will not allow you to leave the palace given your situation, and the political importance of this pregnancy. So you might as well stop arguing and simply accept the hospitality I am offering.'

'Hospitality?' she spat with a flash of her eyes. 'You are turning me into a prisoner!'

'Don't be so melodramatic.' He half laughed, even as tension of a different sort cut through him now, a tension that was born of his own behaviour, and the choices he was now making to protect the baby she purported to know was his.

'Ha,' she said with obvious sarcasm. 'You think my freedom is melodramatic?'

'It is one night,' he lied, 'and from a practical standpoint, it makes sense. You say you are flying out tomorrow. Why waste time in transit?'

India stared up at him with a sense that she was lost at sea, no rescue in sight. She was so angry with him, and it was making her lash out and argue over every small detail, when some of what he said had merit. Besides, she was so tired, the idea of being able to be asleep within minutes was what finally tempted her to concede.

'Fine,' she muttered. 'If you insist.'

His response was to place his palm in the small of her back and guide her towards the door. It was a gesture that meant nothing and yet little lightning bolts of need speared through her, as though her body, filled with a portion of his DNA now, were genetically programmed to recognise and want him, even when her brain was shouting at her to pull away from the man. Only she was tired, and his touch gave her a strength and support she badly needed. At the door, he reached across and took her handbag, hooking it over his shoulder instead, relieving her of the burden of its weight.

She allowed him to do that, because it meant nothing, and it was temporary. In the morning, they'd talk about how this would work, she'd stick firm to the ideas she had for the kind of role that would work for her and their baby, and then she'd leave—putting him, this country, and the whole thing behind her.

But with every step they took, doubts began to plague her. She'd been so sure this was the right thing, but she acknowledged now that she'd given up all of her power by coming here to his country, right into the heart of his palace. Only her fears went way beyond that. Because irrespective of the fact that he was a sheikh and she was not, there was something between them that scared India to death.

She wanted him.

Their bodies were close, brushing as they moved, and it took all of her concentration to remember that she hated him, when her traitorous fingers were itching to reach for his chest, spin him around and feel his warmth against the palms of her hand.

It was all the more reason she had to get this over with and leave. One night with Khalil had been dangerously addictive, any more than that and she wasn't sure she'd ever be able to get him out of her head, and, for the sake of her sanity, she *had* to move on.

CHAPTER SIX

INDIA COULDN'T REMEMBER the last time she'd slept so well. It didn't make sense, with all that loomed over her head, and yet the previous day's exertions, the heat, the mental stress had all combined to mean that as soon as her head hit the pillow, she was in another world. She was not aware of stirring at all through the night, and in the morning, it wasn't nausea that woke her, but the sound of a door clicking across the room. She blinked open her eyes, disorientated by the sight that greeted her. This wasn't her bedroom. It took her a moment to remember exactly where she was, and a moment longer than that to push up to a sitting position and realise that Khalil was standing just inside the door to her enormous guest suite, his arms crossed over his chest, his eyes trained on her with the sort of possessive heat that definitely skittled her ability to think straight.

He wore a suit today, dark trousers, a crisp

white shirt and a jacket that reminded her of the night they'd met. Her mouth felt dry; she looked towards the bedside table, then reached for the glass of water there.

'Good morning.' His voice was like treacle against her nerves.

'What time is it?' she asked, still disorientated.

'Nine o'clock.'

'Nine o'clock?' she repeated, jackknifing out of bed in surprise before remembering that she'd slept in underpants and a singlet top in deference to the desert heat. His eyes skimmed her body and little flames leaped beneath her skin. Oh, how she wished she were less aware of him on a physical level! It would be so much easier to have this conversation if her body weren't willing to betray her at every opportunity. She glared at him to compensate for the direction of her thoughts, then, as an afterthought, dragged the sheet off the bed, wrapping it around her shoulders like a superhero cape.

His smile made her feel like a ridiculous toddler; her expression grew defiant.

'And?' she prompted. 'Is there a reason you've barged in on me?'

His face sobered but she had the sense he was concealing a smile, and that angered her more. 'The doctor will be here soon. I thought you would appreciate a chance to eat something, and dress, before she arrives.'

'What doctor?'

'The gynaecologist,' he said, as though this were something they'd discussed time and time again.

'I don't have a gynaecologist.'

'You do now. Did you want to shower?'

She compressed her lips. 'I don't need to see a doctor.'

'I beg to differ.' He crossed the room, gesturing to the table. It was laden with trays of food and a pot of steaming hot coffee. Her stomach gave a little roll and a hint of nausea spread through her; she looked away again.

'I just want toast or something simple,' she said, then, aware it sounded ungrateful, she explained. 'I've had pretty bad morning sickness. I find it hard to eat much.'

'That explains why you have lost weight, rather than gained it.'

She dipped her head. 'I know people talk about morning sickness being bad, but I had no idea. And it's not just in the mornings, either, it's all day.'

'And that is common in the first trimester?'

'Yes.' Then, suspecting he was actually asking a different question, she expelled a sigh. 'I really don't know how I'm going to convince you that this is your baby.'

His eyes bored into hers, and she wished, more than anything, that he would simply believe her. But Khalil mistrusted her with every fibre of his being, that much was obvious, and this was a pretty important thing to have faith about. She moved to her backpack and lifted out the change of clothes she'd brought.

'I'll shower first,' she said, moving towards the en suite bathroom. Hovering just inside the door, she turned to face him. 'Are you still going to be here?'

'Of course.'

She lifted a brow. 'Great.' If he detected the sarcasm, he didn't react. She took her time showering—the steam felt impossibly good, and the products were the most luxurious, fragrant things she'd ever seen. A far cry from the simple bar soap she used at home for the sake of economy. The rest of the bathroom was just as well appointed, with moisturisers and a hairdryer, even a small selection of nail polishes and face masks. No convenience had been overlooked.

Not for her, obviously.

There had been no notice of her arrival, and certainly no expectation of her being accommodated. This was clearly how guest rooms at the royal palace were kitted out. If India were prone to bitterness, she might have experienced a wave of it to contemplate the disparities and inequities in life. She had become so good at making her toiletries stretch, cutting the bottom off the tube of toothpaste, to squeeze every last bit out, mixing moisturiser with kitchen oil to make it last longer—what must it be like to live in such obvious wealth? Without a care in the world, at least not a financial one. Her head swam when she thought of the bills she had back home—with no way to cover them. But pulling Jackson out of college wasn't an option. She *had* to work out a way through this.

Her hand moved over her stomach in a habit she'd developed. Though she was only eight weeks along, she felt a fierce connection to her baby already, and she knew she would do anything to give them everything she could in life. How was she ever going to be able to care for her brother and her baby?

The dress she'd brought was a simple blue linen sundress, cut on the bias so it was floaty around her slender body, with sleeves that covered just the tops of her arms. She wore minimal make-up when she wasn't working; India applied a hint of lip gloss and mascara now, then, in concession to a face that was pale from the ravages of her hormones—she had no idea when the 'glowing' stage of pregnancy began but she was far from it!—a light dusting of blush on her cheek-bones. Her blonde hair she left down, pulled over one shoulder to keep her neck cool—even now, the sun was high and the day's warmth could be felt penetrating the ancient glass of the palace's windows.

Khalil was sitting at the table when she emerged, his legs spread wide, a large phone in front of him. His face bore a scowl, so she paused, wondering if he would prefer to be left to read whatever was giving him such displeasure alone? Except he'd come to *her* room, and they had only the morning to deal with their situation—she was already counting the minutes to her flight. Escape was imperative. Only once she lifted off the tarmac would she be able to breathe easily again.

As she drew near to the table he looked up, his dark brown eyes lancing her, so she almost lost her footing and tore her gaze away, her breath uneven. What kind of joke was God playing to make this man the only person she'd ever been attracted to?

'Is everything okay?' She nodded towards the phone, taking the seat furthest from him—across the table.

A slightly mocking look in his eyes convinced her that he understood and was amused by her efforts. Heat flushed her face.

'Fine. Just checking over a contract.'

'Is that part of your...job?'

She reached for what looked to be a muffin, sniffing it first and finding that she could tolerate the sweet fragrance—a good sign! It had pieces of fruit and something like cinnamon stirred through it, and it was still warm from the oven. Cutting into it, India added a generous whip of butter, watching as it melted through the middle.

'My job involves many things,' he said with a lift of his shoulders.

'Such as?'

'In less than a year, I will become the head of this state. Already I undertake a great many political tasks on my father's behalf; that will increase once I am crowned.'

Again, India wondered about his father's health, and somehow, she understood what he wasn't saying. She had experience with that particular type of stress, and the euphemisms one used, the words employed to skate about the subject and avoid deeper questioning. The truth was, it was very difficult to discuss a parent's mortality. She didn't push him on the subject.

'I suppose there have been many expectations on you since birth,' she said, wondering what that must have been like. He was born to a unique position, and must have been raised with an awareness of that.

'I have never known any different,' he said, his

eyes regarding her with an intensity that took her breath away. 'And what of you, India? What is it in your life that made you decide to enter into your…vocation?'

Heat stung her cheeks, and she understood the meaning beneath his quietly voiced question. 'I needed a job that was flexible, that paid well. It ticked the boxes.'

She felt his disapproval coming off him in waves but at least he didn't disparage her any further. How could a man with all this understand the position she'd been in?

'I was lucky to find Warm Engagements,' she said, biting into the muffin and swooning a little as the flavours spread through her. It was the first food she'd genuinely enjoyed in weeks, and she took a moment to have a little silent celebration. She washed it down with a whole glass of water, thirsty from the heat of the night, then poured another. 'I had done a little work for them in the past—my best friend's been there for years. I knew it was an agency of quality, the kind of place that didn't stand for what you accused me of,' she insisted. 'And that was important to me. Plus, the pay is really great.'

His expression showed he didn't believe her. She sighed, but what did it matter in the scheme of things? She didn't have to win Khalil over. They weren't going to be friends, or anything to one another whatsoever—they were simply two people who would have a child in common. And surely he'd lose interest in their baby once he'd married and procured legitimate royal heirs right here in Khatrain?

'Anyway, I really just came here to tell you about the baby. I'm happy to see your doctor, if that's important to you, but then I'd like to leave.'

'Your flight is not until the afternoon,' he reminded her softly.

He sounded like himself, but there was an undercurrent to his words that set the hairs at the back of her neck on end. It all seemed…too easy. She'd come to Khatrain to tell him the truth, because she knew the importance of that, but she'd expected him to respond differently. Without fully acknowledging the fear to herself, she realised now that she'd had a niggling worry he might insist on holding her in the country for longer, perhaps until the baby was born, so he could be assured of his parentage. His calm acceptance of her departure didn't ring true. Which meant… She gulped past a lump in her throat, knowing she needed to play it cool, and act totally calm.

'I don't mind hanging around in the airport.'

'Tell me this, then.' His gravelled voice drew her attention back to his face; her stomach swooped. 'What did you expect me to say, when you dropped this bombshell in my lap?'

She took another bite of the muffin to buy time. 'I wasn't sure. I just knew that it was the right thing to do.'

His eyes widened and yet she couldn't understand even a hint of what he was feeling. He was a completely closed book to her.

'And if I say I want nothing to do with you or the baby?'

India dropped her eyes to the table, her father's rejection spearing her sharply, so for a moment she couldn't speak. The idea of their baby, still just a little cluster of cells but growing bigger and stronger every day, having to be born into a world where that kind of rejection was their reality?

'I would accept that, and do everything in my power to shield my child from the pain of your decision.'

She wasn't looking at him, so didn't see the way his jaw tightened, his eyes flashing with surprise.

'What pain might that be?'

Her laugh was hollow, a weak, tremulous sound. 'The pain of knowing their father didn't want to be a part of their life.' She shook her head, reaching for the juice.

Silence prickled around the room, so that when she put her glass on the table and it knocked the edge of her plate, the noise was almost deafening.

'And financially?' he prompted.

Pride kept her silent on that score—he didn't need to know how dreadful her situation was. 'I'll cope,' she promised through gritted teeth. And even though the idea of child support was something she knew to be fair—and certainly given their relative positions—the thought of taking anything from this man, who thought so little of her and might not even want to know her child, was painful to think about.

'You have support?'

Her heart felt heavy. She had *no* support, but again, she kept that to herself, not wanting to reveal anything more to Khalil than was necessary. He wasn't on her side. Whatever she thought she'd felt in him that first night they'd met, he'd shown his true colours since then, and she would give him only the bare minimum details—details that would show him she had no intention of being pushed around nor dictated to by him. 'I'll be fine,' she reiterated firmly. 'There is a hospital near me; I've chosen to have the baby there. Obviously, I will keep you updated as the pregnancy develops and if you want to come and see the baby once he or she is born, then I'll understand.'

'How good of you.' He lifted a coffee cup to his lips and took a drink, his features like stone. The cup was too small and fine for his enormous hands—it looked ridiculous.

'So having a baby without being married means nothing to you?'

A warning siren blared in the back of her mind. Marriage was a topic she saw no sense in discussing. 'Life has a habit of dispensing curve balls.' She pressed a finger into a crumb on the edge of her plate, lifting it to her lips with no idea of the way the small, thoughtless gesture affected the Sheikh. 'I know that I'm not afraid, and that I am resourceful and determined. Our child will *never* lack for anything it needs. I'll make sure of that.'

'That's what I'm afraid of,' he muttered, refilling his coffee.

'What does that mean?'

'I have already seen the lengths you are prepared to go to in order to make a living. What will you do once there is a baby to support? What kind of environment will this child be raised in?'

'A loving one,' she responded, fear snagging in her throat. She had to get out of here. She stood, gripping the back of the chair in both hands, needing the support. 'I will not sit here and be judged by you for having made decisions you cannot possibly fathom. I came here as a courtesy but let me be clear: this is *my* child. I have done my duty and informed you of the fact they exist, but that's where I'm drawing a line. You don't need to be a part of their life and you sure as heck don't get to sit there and lecture me and act as though you're so damn morally superior to me. I will love this baby with all my heart, and that is enough.'

'Except it isn't enough,' he interjected quietly, something sharp in his gaze that stood as a warning to India. The warning siren was blaring louder now. She dug her fingers into the chair back, seeking strength.

'Babies are expensive, and they require care. Who will look after this child if you are working nights? Or is your plan to find some other man and stooge him into marrying you, to help you care for our baby? Because if you think I am having my son or daughter raised by another then you are frankly delusional.'

'That hadn't even entered my mind,' she denied hotly. 'But, as a point of fact, I was raised by my stepfather from the age of four and he is so much more of a father to me than my biological dad ever was. So if I should choose to marry, at some point, that has nothing to do with you.'

'I disagree.'

'You disagree as a matter of habit,' she snapped.

'A habit we share.'

'There is a difference between disagreeing and defending—I am forced to do the latter with you at every turn.'

'If you are defensive of your lifestyle then that is a question for your conscience.'

She ground her teeth together. 'I'm not defending my lifestyle, damn it! I am defending what you *believe* my lifestyle to be; there's a difference.'

He held up a hand, in a clearly authoritative manner. 'Let us not discuss your—profession. It is clearly upsetting to you and, given your condition, that should be avoided. Besides, it doesn't matter now. You are pregnant, and whatever happened before is irrelevant to the future of this baby. Okay?'

No! It's not okay! She wanted to scream the denial at him, to tell him she didn't want to live in a world where he thought her capable of what he'd accused her. Where he could reduce what they'd shared down to a financial transaction. Her pride hurt with the knowledge that she hadn't been able to simply tear up the cheque he'd written her, but without that money, she could never have afforded to come to Khatrain and tell him the truth.

A knock sounded at the door, making any response impossible, as Khalil stood and moved with his long, confident gait towards it. He drew it inwards and a woman entered, followed by a male with a large trolley.

'Your Highness.' She bowed towards the Sheikh, and the man behind the doctor did the same.

'This way.' His voice was grim as he gestured towards India. She felt like a naughty schoolgirl, being dragged before the headmaster. At the same time, even this brought her a hint of pleasure, because seeing a doctor in America was a luxury beyond her means. She'd done an at-home pharmacy test to confirm her pregnancy, then another to confirm the confirmation, but she had been waiting until closer to twenty weeks to book a hospital appointment for a scan.

'Dr Abasha.' Khalil gestured to India. 'India McCarthy.'

'How do you do?' Dr Abasha's smile was kind, and India warmed to her immediately.

'Thank you for seeing me,' India murmured.

'Of course, it is my honour.' She turned to Khalil. 'Is there somewhere private I can speak to the patient?'

India had to hide a smile; it was clear Khalil didn't like being excluded, but after a moment's hesitation, he exited the room.

'I take it you've done a home pregnancy test?' the doctor asked, reaching into her briefcase and withdrawing another such test.

'Yes. Two of them.'

'Well, they are almost always accurate, but this one is a little different—it will tell me the amount of hCG—the pregnancy hormone—in your system at the moment. It's useful for many things, including dating the pregnancy.'

India's heart dropped to her toes. This woman knew what her job was: to confirm—or maybe even to deny?—that the baby was the Sheikh's. The idea of a protracted fight over paternity made her stomach ache—she would never do it. There would be too much risk of publicity, and she couldn't have her baby ever discovering that India had needed to fight for the father to acknowledge their life.

'Okay,' she said. 'No problems.'

When she was finished with the pregnancy test, she carried it out to the doctor, who regarded it with a smile at first, and then a small frown. 'You say you are eight weeks along?'

India nodded. She knew the exact date of conception, of course. But the doctor's countenance gave her some cause for concern. 'Yes. Why? Is there a problem?'

'Could there be some confusion with dates?'

'Definitely not.'

Dr Abasha took the pregnancy test and placed it on the trolley, then switched the light on so a monitor on the top tray came to life. 'Come and have a lie-down. Let's do a scan to see what's going on.'

India's eyes grew wide. 'Isn't it too early?'

'We'll see. At eight weeks, a dating scan should be possible.'

Under different circumstances, she might have felt excited, but there was a look of concern on the doctor's face that made India hold her breath.

Her dress had buttons down the front so she undid several in the middle and lay on the bed as Dr Abasha moved the trolley closer. 'Would you like me to get His Highness?'

'No,' India denied quickly. 'Let me see first, please.'

Dr Abasha hesitated a moment before nodding, applying a cold, wet goo to India's belly. 'Lie still,' she said. 'This will be a little uncomfortable.'

She moved the wand around, her eyes on the screen as she shifted positions, her fingertips clicking buttons before she peered closer at the image.

'Is there a problem?' India asked, after what felt like for ever.

Dr Abasha's eyes met India's. 'Stay here, madam.'

India's heart was racing, worry clutching at her, as Dr Abasha left the room and returned, a moment later, with Khalil. His eyes met India's and she felt her own worries reflected in his.

'Please, just tell me what's going on,' India begged, pushing up onto her elbows, uncaring that her belly was still exposed and covered in translucent blue syrup.

'The dating scan confirms that you are eight weeks pregnant, madam, congratulations.'

Khalil's eyes bored into hers, and India's heart tripped over itself, the triumph of that moment dwarfed by something else entirely. She swallowed past a lump in her throat, turning back to the doctor. 'And the baby's okay?'

'I was interested by your high levels of hCG— much higher than one would expect at this stage of a pregnancy, hence the dating scan.'

'Do high levels of hCG indicate a problem?' India asked, panic overtaking her now.

'Not in this case,' Dr Abasha said with a smile. 'Tell me, do twins run in your family?'

India's jaw dropped and she shook her head, trying to make sense first of the doctor's implication and then of her question.

'My mother is a twin,' Khalil said. 'And her mother.'

'And your children,' the doctor said with a grin, as though this were purely good news.

'Oh, my God.' India sat up straight now, staring at the wall opposite. 'Twins?' She squeezed her eyes shut, her first reaction of sheer delight quickly being overtaken by stress. One child had been scary enough, but two? On her own? And all her bravado seemed to crumple at once, so she had no faith in herself and her resourcefulness, she saw only an enormous, insurmountable wall.

'Thank you, Doctor. What do we do now?'

'You've really already done the important thing,' the doctor said with a wink, then apparently sensed the tone of the room and sobered. 'I will bring some pregnancy vitamins to you later today, as well as information on diet and lifestyle habits to support a healthy pregnancy. Twin pregnancies are generally considered higher risk than single, though in someone of your age and obvious good health, I am not concerned. I'll schedule another scan for you at twelve weeks.'

'Higher risk as in...something might go wrong?' India asked, latching onto the question, feeling Khalil's eyes on her.

'There is a slightly higher risk, yes,' the doctor said gently. 'The first trimester is when a miscarriage is most likely—but you are already eight weeks. It is also likely the twins will be born early—anywhere from thirty-six weeks, sometimes even sooner.'

Perspiration dampened India's brow and she pressed a hand to her stomach, a fierce need to do whatever she could to protect her babies rushing through her.

'What can I do?' she asked.

'Nothing.' Dr Abasha smiled kindly. 'Eat well, get plenty of rest, avoid stress, relax. And wait.'

India closed her eyes, because such simple instructions were almost impossible for her to follow. Her life back home was not relaxing, stress was a constant companion, she wasn't sleeping and as for eating well—it depended on what she could afford.

'Okay, sure,' she said, fighting back tears. 'I can do that.' For her babies, she'd find a way. And she knew what that would mean. Selling the family home. She'd been determined to hold onto it for Jackson, and when she'd found out that she was pregnant, the idea of raising her babies in the home she'd lived in with her parents had made her feel that they would be a part of the baby's life, but it was more important to take care of her pregnancy in the here and now.

By selling the home, she could free up enough cash to buy a small apartment that she'd own outright. That would alleviate some worries. But what about the medical bills and Jackson's college fees? It would quickly chew through the capital, so whatever she had to spend on an apartment would quickly diminish.

She was conscious of Khalil walking the doctor out, thanking her for her time before closing the door, pressing his back to it. Once they were alone, she realised, belatedly, that she hadn't corrected the doctor on something.

'I won't be here this afternoon,' India said quietly, standing on legs that were so full of adrenaline and surprise they wobbled a little. She had to get out of Khatrain, and fast. Something about the discovery she was carrying twins made everything seem more urgent—and dangerous.

Khalil's brow lifted in a silent encouragement for her to continue.

'The doctor said she'd bring some vitamins and information to me, but I won't be here. Do you think she could come back sooner?'

'I think,' Khalil said, his voice quiet yet determined, 'that your place is now in Khatrain. Not only will you be here this afternoon, India, you will be here from now on.'

CHAPTER SEVEN

IT WAS HER worst fears—fears she hadn't fully acknowledged to herself until this moment—confirmed. She stared at him, shaking her head, even when she knew there had always been a risk of this. Why had she thought she could give him this news and then leave again? What kind of fool was she?

He crossed his arms over his chest, everything firming into place with the strength and certainty of lightning, bolting towards the earth.

'You're pregnant with my *children*. Clearly you cannot go back to America.'

'I'm sorry, that is certainly *not* clear to me. What difference does it make that they're twins?' She stared at him in that way she had, as though he were so far beneath her, her blue eyes narrowing scathingly. 'Or is it simply that you believe me now that a doctor has confirmed their gestational age?'

'The doctor's confirmation was important,'

he said unapologetically. 'Anyone in my position would seek the same assurance.'

'And my word wasn't enough?'

Strangely though, Khalil hadn't questioned the honesty of her statement until she had suggested that he might doubt her. Then, it had been easy to believe she was lying to him—after all, Fatima had already greased the wheels there, her dishonesty and ultimately viciously mercenary behaviour making it impossible for him to trust women, particularly when it came to children.

'I have the confirmation I wanted,' he said, as though that was all that mattered. 'And now we must focus on the future.'

Indignation fired in her eyes so he was tempted to sweep her into his arms and kiss it away, reminding her that before there was this anger between them, a different kind of passion had flared.

'I *have* been focussing on the future,' she said through gritted teeth, looking around the room with a hint of panic in her eyes then striding towards the sofa, where she'd discarded a shirt at some point during her stay. She lifted it up and stuffed it into her backpack, then disappeared into the bathroom, returning with a small, zipped bag that she also added to the backpack. 'I've been focussed on nothing but the future since I learned of this pregnancy, but that future is not here in Khatrain. I'm going home.'

'The sooner you start to think of this as your home, the better.'

Her lips parted and she stared at him as though she couldn't fathom this response—as though it had never occurred to her that he might fight to be a part of the children's lives.

'You said you would do whatever it took to give your child everything you could in life; are you surprised to discover I feel the same way?'

'Yes, frankly,' she said with a shake of her head, as if to dispel the very idea. 'I'm not here because I want you in their lives! I came because—'

'You thought I should know. Yes, you have said this, many times. But what did you think I would do with that knowledge, *azeezi*?'

'I—don't know.' She zipped up her backpack and lifted it over one shoulder, but the gesture— while valiant—lacked certainty, and her trademark defiance was nowhere to be seen. The truth was, she'd feared this response, but she'd told herself it wasn't possible. She'd lied to herself, because a desire to do the right thing had outweighed her self-preservation instincts. Or was it something else that had motivated her to fly to Khatrain? Had she actually hoped—but, no. India would not allow her thoughts to go in such a mortifying direction. She didn't want any part of what he was suggesting!

'I will be Sheikh of Khatrain—did you think I would allow my child to be raised in America? That I would simply visit from time to time, when I happened to be in the area? Did you think this pregnancy would mean so little to me that I would not turn my life on its head to accommodate it—and you?'

Her lip trembled and he felt, unmistakably, pity for her.

'I thought you wouldn't want it,' she said softly, and shock split through him.

'I thought you'd be angry at me for having conceived. I thought you'd offer money for me to disappear, and that you'd marry someone else soon enough and have royal heirs all of your own, so that you wouldn't want the embarrassment of our illegitimate child hanging around your neck.'

He stared at her in shock. 'Nothing you have described is what I feel, believe me.' His eyes narrowed though as he replayed her statement in his mind. 'Did you want money? Is that why you came?'

Sadness shaped her features. 'No.' Her voice was hollow. 'And I wouldn't have taken it, even if you'd offered it.'

'Even for the baby?'

'Not unless it was a matter of life and death,'

she said emphatically. 'Children don't need much beyond love and that I am well able to provide.'

Admiration flared in his gut, and something else too: gratitude. Because the most important trait he could ask for in the mother of his children was that she would want to protect them with her life, and India clearly felt that in spades.

'This is a decision you no longer have to make.'

'You mean it's a decision I no longer *get* to make,' she corrected, fidgeting with her fingers. 'If I stay in Khatrain, it will be because you've forced me.'

'How about we try a different word?' he said as he crossed towards her, lifting the backpack off her shoulder and placing it on the floor. 'What if we speak of persuasion instead?'

'You have not persuaded me. You've dictated to me.'

His look alone silenced her.

'You cannot afford one baby, let alone twins. Your debts are monumental, and you lost your job at the agency shortly after our night together.'

Her eyes were like saucers in her face, her skin blanching pale. 'How did you know?'

'That doesn't matter.'

'It matters to me! Have you been spying on me?'

'Naturally I did my research,' he said. 'I thought someone might have taken a photograph of us kissing at the bar, remember? I wanted to be prepared if the story broke in the papers.' He raked her face with his eyes, his expression grim. 'You are in no position to fight me.'

'And yet I would, with all that I am.'

'It would never be enough.' He moved closer, near enough to touch. 'You are in my country, where we play purely by my rules. Even if we weren't, I have the means—and motivation—to pursue custody of our children through the highest courts in your country. And I would win, India. Your vocational choices make that a given.'

'Damn it, Khalil, I'm not what you think I am.'

'Even if that is true, working as an escort is still enough to put doubt into a judge's mind.'

Her lips parted on a whoosh of hurt and he felt a stirring in his gut, a yearning that spread through him like wildfire, so he caught her face in his hands and held her right where she was.

'But beyond that, there is a part of you that doesn't want to fight what I am suggesting. There is a part of you that wants to stay here with me, isn't there, India?'

Her eyes were like pools of doubts, but they were also awash with desire, so much he could swim in it. He stroked her lower lip, and felt her tremble beneath his touch, the pulse point at the base of her throat visible beneath her translucent skin.

'I found it impossible to resist you that night, and that same desire flashes through me now, even after—' he shook his head. 'What kind of fool does that make me?'

He saw hurt in her eyes right before he kissed her, and he blanked it from his mind. He didn't want to wound her. He was only being honest. And in that moment, all he honestly wanted was to kiss her until he felt sane again.

She was breathless with the pleasure of his kiss, its unexpected nature catching her off guard, so she was completely lost to him, her knees sagging her body forward, and it was the most natural thing for his arm to clamp around her waist, holding her to him.

Fight him. Fight this!

Her brain was screaming at her, warning her that within pleasure lay the potential for so much pain, and yet they were bonded, the two of them; bonded by babies and something else, an undeniable force that held them together, so that when he lifted her and carried her to the bed, she didn't even think about saying anything to resist him.

She didn't want to. It was selfish and short-sighted but India's craving for Khalil usurped everything else. He undressed her quickly, pausing only to undo his own belt and trousers before he separated her thighs with his knee then pushed into her, kissing her as he possessed her body. She groaned at the immediate sensation of relief then white-hot pleasure, his possession of her swift and urgent, the same need rushing through them both, overpowering them, making speech and sense unnecessary. There was only this.

His fingers weaved with hers, pinning her hands above her head as he moved, trapping her. His other hand roamed her breast, cupping it as he kissed her and thrust deep and hard, faster and faster as their need grew to the point where neither could bear it, neither could fight it: they clung to one another as they exploded, pleasure a burst of light that, for a moment, pushed aside the dark.

Khalil's body weight on top of hers was blissful, but only for a moment. Reality began to push against her and regrets were not far behind. This situation was complicated enough without having brought sex right back into it. India's breathing slowed and his weight became impossible to bear, so she pushed at his chest, rolling out from beneath him and standing, lifting a hand to her forehead and shaking her head.

'That shouldn't have happened.'

There was no regret in his face, only determination. Had he planned to seduce her? To prove a point?

'No,' he said simply, so she realised she'd asked the questions aloud.

'Then what the heck…?'

'I meant what I said. Whatever drew us together that night still exists between us. Nothing that happened since has changed our desire.'

'But it has for me! Everything is different now.'

She had the satisfaction of seeing his eyes darken with something like doubt, but it was gone again almost instantly, arrogance back in place.

'The fact we have this chemistry is a bonus, India. Our marriage needn't be a disaster—we can share this, and our children. Many people have wed for much less.'

Her jaw dropped, her mind too spongy to make sense of what he was saying. 'Did you just say—our marriage?'

'Of course. What else did you think I meant when I said you would stay in Khatrain?'

'I thought you meant until I'd had the babies.'

'And then what?' he asked, sitting up. 'Did you believe I would pack you off to America, out of our babies' lives?'

'You'll forgive me if I don't give you much benefit of the doubt,' she responded, her eyes devouring his naked form even as she tried to pull away from him.

'You were wrong.' He ignored her barb. 'I meant for you, and the children, to remain here.

Obviously we must marry, to ensure their place in the line of succession.'

It was all too much. India shook her head, looking around for the time. She could still make her flight. She just had to convince Khalil that was in everyone's best interests—she needed him to see sense.

'You believe that I've been engaged in the kind of career that no one in your kingdom would *ever* accept. What if we were to marry and your suspicions hit the papers? You were worried enough when it was a simple kiss in a bar, but marriage?'

'That is a consideration,' he said seriously. 'But it's a risk we must take.'

'What about your father?' She pushed, desperate.

His lips tightened. 'There is no option but to marry—for the sake of our children.'

'You're not listening to me. I don't need your help. I can raise my children in the States, on my own.'

'But they are my children too, India, and I will fight for them with every last breath in my body. I will not allow them to be raised away from me. So what option do we have then?'

Consternation struck her in the middle. She looked around for her clothes—discarded at the foot of the bed—and pulled on her dress, preferring not to have this conversation while she was stark naked, her body still covered in red patches from his stubble and touch.

'Let me put it this way instead,' he said slowly, once she was dressed. 'The line of succession in Khatrain is quite specific. On my thirtieth birthday—in a matter of months—I am to inherit the throne. I will be crowned Sheikh, but only if I am married. It is a peculiar requirement of our country's constitution. I have known for a long time that I must choose a bride and marry swiftly. If we were to do this your way, and not marry, I still would not permit you to leave Khatrain until the children were born, at which point I would demand that they remain here. In the meantime, I would be forced to marry one of the women my advisors have urged me to consider, and that woman, my wife and Sheikha, would be a step-mother to our children. Is that the future you want?'

She gasped, hot, bright lights flashing in her eyes at the awful picture he painted.

'Or,' he continued, his voice husky, his accent thick, 'you could accept my proposal. Marry me and we will raise the children together. You would live the life of royalty, my kingdom would be your kingdom, the homes I have around the globe yours to enjoy, a fleet of jets at your disposal to travel home and see family any time you wished. And there would be this,' he reminded her, standing and placing his arms on her hips, holding her tight against his taut body. 'A marriage that meets both of our needs, yes?'

'No,' she whispered, shaking her head, even as the strength of his argument was impossible to fault. How could she deny what he was offering? And what he was implying would happen if she didn't agree? He was carving out a place for her in his life, in royal life, and, most importantly, in their children's lives. The alternative was not hard to imagine: she would be sidelined at first and excluded eventually, her children raised without her.

But marrying a man she didn't love? Who despised her? Since she'd watched her mother fall in love with her stepfather, India had known she wanted exactly that for herself—true, everlasting love. A proper family. That certainty had only solidified as she'd continued to witness her parents' happiness over the years.

Marrying for love was a luxury no longer open to her. She wanted—more than anything—for her children to be near to her. That had to override everything else.

'And what will you tell your people about me? More importantly, your parents?'

'My parents will be so glad to know I'm engaged. They will not ask questions beyond that.'

He made it sound so simple, but it wasn't. Marriage to Khalil was paved with danger. If the last half-hour had taught her anything it was that she was monumentally weak where he was concerned. What would it be like when they were husband and wife?

It was all too much to consider—she needed more time, a chance to breathe and think this through. But Khalil was staring at her, his mind made up. And on one score, he was perfectly right. She was in *his* country. His word was law.

'Getting married is extreme,' she said, her voice juddering.

'On the contrary, it is sensible.'

She analysed their situation from every angle, trying to see her way through this, to imagine a different future. But all roads led back to the truth: they were tied together already. Was there any harm in formalising it? And yet, still she clung to the idea of more time, a chance to be sure she wouldn't live to regret this decision. Lost in thought, she didn't notice as he moved closer, his hand lifting to her cheek, cupping it. 'And it is not as though our marriage won't have a silver lining. It's clear we share this desire.'

She bit down on her lip as her body responded to his nearness, his touch, overriding her momentary uncertainty. His eyes probed hers and she bit back a sigh, because she wanted to lift up and kiss him, but as soon as she did that, she knew what would happen—again. They couldn't simply tumble into bed together every time they got close. This conversation was too important to be overpowered by their very mutual desire. India forced herself to step back, away from him and temptation, but it did nothing to tamp down on the slick of heat between her legs. She looked away, frustrated at her body's response.

'You don't understand,' she murmured. 'My parents loved each other. I've always wanted that.'

His eyes sparkled, a hint of challenge in their depths. 'It's unrealistic.'

'A loving marriage? You're kidding, right?'

'It's unrealistic for us, in this circumstance.'

She clamped her lips, biting back whatever she'd been intending to say.

'You should be aware that our marriage contract will include a financial arrangement. It's standard for royal marriages.'

Sadness welled inside her—a sadness born of his beliefs. Why didn't he see who she really was? Why didn't he accept her version of events? She wanted to shout at him that she didn't want his money, that he could take his fortune and run straight to hell with it, but the truth was, if she remained in Khatrain, she would need access to funds immediately to cover costs back home. There was a small amount left in her account, which would pay for upcoming utilities, but Jackson's college fees were due before long and India would need… She dug her fingernails into her palms to stop tears from filling her eyes. She would need to accept his payment, again. Her pride was stripped to pieces.

'How much?' The words were whispered, sadness thickening the consonants.

'And now I have your interest?'

'I'm just curious,' she lied, as though it weren't vitally important to her.

'Naturally. What amount do you think would be fair?' he prompted, arms folded over his chest. 'It would help, of course, if I knew your going rate—then we could simply multiply that out to cover a lifetime.'

'Don't.' She squeezed her eyes shut, anguished. She hated what he thought of her! And worse, that she was now living up to it, by accepting any kind of marriage settlement.

'Why not?' He sighed heavily. 'Why can't you at least own your decisions, India?'

Her stomach looped. He couldn't possibly think any worse of her. The truth was, she knew exactly the amount she needed—enough to cover Jackson's degree. She would sooner sell the house than ask this man for a cent more—as much as that would pain her. It was her family home, but her mother would have understood. She wouldn't debase herself for a physical possession, but for Jackson? So he could stay at college, even when she was over here? She couldn't leave him stranded. He had to be taken care of; her parents would have expected that of her.

'I need one hundred thousand American dollars,' she muttered, without meeting his eyes, so she didn't see the surprise that flashed in them—surprise, because his marriage contract with Fatima had stalled at the point she'd sought ten million dollars on the day of their marriage, and a generous annuity thereafter.

'I know it seems like a lot.' She continued to stare at the ground, hating this situation with all her heart.

'And what do you need this sum for, India?'

Her skin grew pale. She looked away, the awful truth of her financial situation like a lump in her throat.

'It's…personal.'

'So personal you cannot share it with your fiancé?'

Fiancé…! She squeezed her eyes closed. Was she really going to do this?

'Does it matter?' she murmured eventually.

'No.' Contempt fired in the word and her stomach dropped. 'Was there anything else?'

She was on a sinking ship, unable to find a life vest. She looked around, panicked, her mind in a spin. But yes, there was one other consideration, the most important one of all perhaps.

'I think we should wait another month to announce our engagement.'

'No. We must marry immediately; within days.'

'Let me finish,' she insisted. 'You heard what the doctor said. The first trimester carries a higher risk of miscarriage. I hope and pray with all my heart that we are blessed with two healthy babies in seven months' time, but if we're not, if anything happens, then there's no point in... the marriage between us...wouldn't make sense.'

'I also heard the doctor say that your risks are low,' he reminded her.

'Low, but not nil. It's a simple precaution. You've made it perfectly clear that I'm far from the ideal bride. Why risk upsetting everyone if it's not necessary?'

His expression was inscrutable, his handsome, symmetrical face as still as if it had been carved from granite.

'It makes sense,' she said softly. 'We'll wait a month, and then, if everything looks good, and this still makes sense... I'll marry you, Khalil.'

CHAPTER EIGHT

KHALIL LEANED LOW to the stallion's mane, his eyes focussed on the waving lines of the horizon, the early morning sun already beating down on his back. He rode hard, the wind rushing past him a balm he needed, the freedom of the desert one of the few things that could bring him a sense of relief.

Every day since India had arrived, he'd done this—pursuing the dawn in a fruitless attempt to catch it, pitting his power and strength against the elements of the universe. He wasn't seeking victory though, so much as attempting to outrun his thoughts.

His engagement to Fatima had been a disaster. For one thing, he'd believed himself in love, which was, he realised now, just about the worst reason one could have for getting married. Particularly a wedding of this sort. He didn't need a wife he loved, he needed one who would provide him with heirs, and in this way, India was perfect. Two children already on the way meant the order of succession would be protected.

But he had been careless with Fatima—because he'd loved her. He'd trusted her and believed her: mistakes he would never make again. It was the only explanation for why he'd palmed off the arranging of the marriage contracts to his lawyers rather than overseeing negotiations himself. He'd presumed Fatima would want nothing—that she would know that, as his wife, she could have whatever she wished. It hadn't been enough, though. Her greed had known no bounds, and as her list of demands had grown more and more outrageous, his legal team had sought to protect him, with no idea that she had something in her belly he would have paid his entire kingdom to keep safe.

He leaned lower, murmuring quietly to the horse so his ears pricked and he began to move faster, cooperating with the Sheikh's commands.

A week ago, India had arrived in Khatrain, and since she'd provisionally agreed to marry him, he'd steered clear of her. But that, he realised, was a mistake. If he'd been more involved in the negotiations with Fatima, he might have been able to prevent what had happened. He should have been able to save their baby. He would never forgive himself for the fact that his carelessness had led to that tragedy—he had to do whatever he could to protect *these* babies, here and now.

He would care for India, he would manage their marriage negotiations personally, and then, on the day of the deadline she had imposed, they would marry.

Discomfort pressed against him. He had never imagined he'd be in this position. He was a highly sought-after bachelor, his bed never empty for long, the prospect of marrying him something many princesses and heiresses had made clear they wished to fulfil. India was not one of them.

And that bothered him.

What was he expecting? That she'd jump at the chance to marry a man who'd scorned her the morning after they'd slept together? That she'd ignore the way he'd spoken to her, ignore the fact he'd treated her like—

He made a low growling sound, his frustration bursting from him. He hated how they'd met. He hated that he'd used her, and that she'd used him. He hated the way he'd spoken to her the morning after they'd slept together, but, more than that, he hated the idea of her using her beautiful body to seduce men purely for financial gain.

And yet, what if Ethan had lied?

The question had been hammering away at him since he'd left America. What if he was wrong? What if she was telling the truth? The sun shifted, rays of warmth beating across his back. He clamped down on his naïve desire to believe her, or even to set aside what he knew of her career. He'd believed in Fatima, and it had cost him the world. He would never be so stupid again. India was to be the mother of his children, but he could never allow himself to trust her. Too much was at stake.

But that didn't mean he could keep ignoring her either—or pretending to ignore her. No purpose was served by running away from her—if he wanted to get her out of his mind, he needed to keep her in his life, in his bed, so that he no longer spent every waking minute craving her to the point of distraction… They were to marry, and the sooner he found a way to live with that— and her—the better.

India disconnected the call with Jackson, a frown on her face. She hated lying to her little brother, but it was for the best. Until she was absolutely certain that she was marrying Khalil, and staying in Khatrain, she didn't see any point in bringing him up to speed. It was just easier to pretend she was still in New York, that life was continuing as normal—or in their new normal, at least.

A knock sounded at her door, startling India out of her thoughts. She put down her phone on the tabletop and stood, just as the door opened and Khalil strode in—but not as she'd ever seen him! He wore loose linen pants, long to the ankle, and his chest was bare, moist with perspiration. His hair was damp, and there was an intensity in his eyes that spread fire to her core. India hadn't seen him in a week, and her body ached for him, so seeing him in her room, dressed like this, was enough to shoot her pulse into overdrive, big time.

'Khalil.' Her voice was hoarse. She stood exactly where she was, even as he began to move towards her and her first instinct was to jolt her legs into action and touch him. The instinct shocked her; she mentally bolted her feet to the floor. 'Is something the matter?'

'Yes.'

Was it possibly he was regretting their arrangement? She stood perfectly still, watching as he strode towards her, but with every step he took, an answering thud landed in her heart, so her pulse was thick and thready by the time he reached her. His eyes furrowed, as though he were lost in thought, his expression inscrutable. He had six freckles across his cheeks, barely recognisable because of the depth of his complexion, but up close she could see them and they mesmerised her.

'This isn't working.'

She swallowed hard. 'What's not?'

'Ignoring you. It won't work.'

Her pulse jumped.

'If we're going to get married, we need to act like it.'

She ignored the torrent of adrenaline and desire that tore through her, aiming to keep a restrained, cool expression on her face. 'Meaning?'

'Meaning we have to be seen together.'

Disappointment seared her; she blinked away, and he made a throaty sound of understanding. Damn it, why was she so easy to read?

'Publicly, but also we must be together privately. It's the only way.'

'We can wait three weeks. Until we know for sure—'

'Can we?' His lips formed a grim smile. 'Is that what you want?'

He scanned her face, not waiting for an answer.

'Or have you been thinking of me this week as I have you? Have you been tortured each night, wanting me to kiss you, to touch you? Have you touched yourself, imagining it was me?'

Heat exploded in her cheeks. She looked away from him, even as her body leaned forward, traitorous, needy body. Her nipples tingled, silently begging for his touch, and, as though they were connected in some way, he lifted his hands, cupping them, catching their weight and brushing his thumbs over her nipples. She tilted her head back, stars dancing against her eyelids.

It was madness, but a madness she had wanted

all week, a touch she needed, even when she hated herself for that.

'We are not marrying for love, but that doesn't mean our marriage need be empty.'

She blinked, his words like a hammer against ice, so she straightened, staring at him, but he moved quickly, kneeling before her, catching the hem of her skirt in his hands and pushing it up as his eyes met hers, taunting her, teasing her, challenging her to reject him. But she didn't— she couldn't. She was spellbound, desire throbbing in her belly. He drew her underpants down slowly, the feel of his palms on her legs sending shock waves of need through her, so she tilted her head back again.

When he kissed her sex, she cried out, the touch so personal and perfect, so unlike anything she'd ever known, that she almost couldn't bear it. Her fingers drove into his hair, tightening around its lengths, a whimper in the base of her throat as his tongue lashed her most sensitive cluster of nerves until she was tumbling into an abyss of delight, her cries ringing out in the room, loud and fast, her hands wrenching his hair until the waves of torturous release eased and she could breathe once more. He stood, something like satisfaction glinting in his eyes, and then he scooped her up, carrying her through the enormous suite and into the bedroom.

'This was real,' he said, and it made no sense, but she didn't have time to question him, because he was undressing, staring at her, as though she were a puzzle he needed to understand. A moment later, his knee separated her legs and his arousal was pushing into her warm, moist core. She arched her back, calling his name out, the taste of it in her mouth perfection, everything about this moment perfection.

His body played hers like a maestro. His mouth tormented her nipples as he thrust into her, hard and fast, then slowly, pulling her pleasure back so that it built to an ultimate, unruly crescendo, each time such pleasure pain in the nearness of her release. He was prolonging their mutual release, and frustration at his mastery clipped through India, so suddenly she pushed at his chest, rolling him onto his back. His eyes caught hers for a moment, surprise obvious, and she grinned as she straddled him, moaning at the delight of it, moving her hips to her own tempo, moving her hands over her breasts as the wave built and built and she rode it towards the crest. His hands dug into her hips, moving her faster, holding her lower, and he bucked as she moved, so their bodies morphed and exploded as one, their cries mingled, the air in the room explosive with the pleasure they felt.

India could barely think afterwards. She stayed

where she was, focussing on her breathing, on the tingling that ran through her body, the throbbing between her legs, the beauty of the man beneath her, the rightness of what they'd just done, even when everything else was such an abject mess, and she realised she didn't feel the regret she had thought she might. She was sure it would come, but for now she wanted to glory in being with him, with the fact she'd taken control and driven him over the edge, with how perfectly their bodies worked together.

'See, India? Whatever else happens in our marriage, we have this. It is enough.'

She wished he wouldn't talk. Their bodies spoke fine for both of them; words ruined everything.

But he *had* spoken and her brain had clicked back into gear, so she had no choice but to respond. 'Is it? I always thought marriages were about love and respect.'

'A childish fantasy,' he murmured, indolently running a hand over her breast, his eyes following the gesture with possessive intent.

'How can you say that?' She shook her head, thinking of her parents' marriage, or everything she knew to be true. 'Haven't you ever been in love?'

'That's irrelevant. *We* are not in love, and never will be, but it doesn't matter.'

She opened her mouth to argue with that, but his finger brushed the flesh between her legs, sparking a bolt of lightning in her belly. She stared at him, and he moved his fingers again, his gaze locked to hers.

Damn it, he knew exactly how to pleasure her, and he did so now, stirring her to fever pitch all over again, before rolling her onto her back, kissing her as he moved his fingers, so when she crested over the wave this time, she was breathless and exhausted, and totally absorbed by sensual pleasure.

She looked like a woman who'd been made love to so thoroughly she could barely speak. He stood, scanning her beautiful body, stepping away from the bed with regret. He'd thought sleeping with her would ease the ache in his gut, the ever-present need, but having opened the floodgates, he simply wanted more of her. He wanted to shower with her, to run the sponge over her body, feeling her soapy and wet beneath his hands, to kiss her, naked, as water ran over them both…

'There is an event tonight. I usually take a date. Come with me.'

She flipped her head to face him, a frown on her lips. He moved towards her, kissing her quickly, so the frown disappeared. 'It's a formal affair. I'll send a stylist to help you prepare.'

He dressed, watching her, waiting for the inevitable argument, because India so often liked to find a flaw in his plans. But she stayed silent, her eyes on him, for so long that it didn't make sense.

'Okay?'

She nodded, but something was clearly wrong.

'What is it?'

Tightness began to coil in his gut. Guilt. They'd both wanted—needed—the release of their coming together, but was she regretting it now? It was a doubt he'd never felt with a woman before.

'It makes sense,' she said eventually, her eyes latching to his. 'If we're going to marry in a few weeks, it will be less…dramatic…if there's some evidence that we actually knew one another prior to the wedding. A date is a good idea.'

'I'm glad you agree.' Even when he'd half been looking forward to convincing her a little more…

'And in private,' he said, moving closer to the bed, his whole body craving her, wanting to lie at her back and hold her close, to simply feel her pressed against him. 'At night, you will be mine, India. We'd be fools to ignore the one good thing this marriage has going for it.'

She swallowed and looked away, so he couldn't tell how she was feeling. 'Three good things,' she said, eventually, when he was about to turn and walk to the door. He waited for her to continue, his breath held.

'The babies,' she reminded him. 'If it weren't for them, we'd never have seen one another again. It's because of them that we're marrying.'

He nodded, and left the room, wondering at the hollow sensation in his gut that simply wouldn't quit.

'Who will be there tonight?' she asked, as the car slowed down at traffic lights, anxiety thickening her blood.

'Dignitaries, film stars, politicians, some diplomats and artists.' He spoke with cold detachment, as though they hadn't made love earlier, as though they were strangers who barely knew one another. 'The gallery is renowned throughout Europe and the Middle East.'

'Are these people your friends?'

'Some are,' he said, but she had the feeling he wasn't being completely honest with her. 'My cousin will be there—Astrid el Abdul. She is a few years younger than me, and a woman of great integrity. I will introduce the two of you. If I am busy, she will take care of you.'

Her smile was lopsided. 'I don't need to be taken care of—you might have forgotten but I'm quite experienced at mingling with strangers at fancy events.'

'The kind of mingling you indulged in in the past will not be tolerated here, remember?'

She looked away from him, her smile dying. 'So Astrid is actually some kind of babysitter for me?'

'If necessary, she will be.'

India bit down on her lip. 'I don't know what I can do to make you believe me,' she said softly, shaking her head at the futility of that. 'I was never that kind of escort.'

He stared at her, his eyes probing hers, and she waited, because for a moment it almost seemed as if he believed her, or wanted to believe her, and she desperately needed that. She didn't know how they could really make their marriage work if he bought into such lies about her. But after a moment, he shrugged, a careless, throwaway gesture, and looked to the window beyond her. 'It doesn't matter any more. We've put the past in the past. Our children are the future.'

But it did matter! India reached across to touch him, and his eyes dropped to the gesture, consternation on his face, so she withdrew her hand abruptly. Were there rules for this too? That they could touch in the bedroom, but not beyond it? Ice filled her heart. She looked away, nodding once, just as the car pulled to a stop outside a modern building on the edge of one of the canals she'd spied from the plane. It was illuminated by red spotlights, and enormous posters were hung from the windows proclaiming the benefit. A score of paparazzi stood waiting, roped off the event, kept separate from the guests.

His hand on her chin surprised her, and as he drew her face back to his she didn't resist. 'I have never wanted a woman as I've wanted you.'

'Is that supposed to make me feel good?'

'It's a start,' he said, with a frustrated jerk of his head. 'We're both working this out as we go along. I don't want to hurt you, but nor do I want to lie to you. I'm not going to pretend to feel something for you that I don't, I won't act as though I care for you or am falling in love with you, simply to placate you. I'm offering a relationship that works for me; you have to decide if it works for you.'

CHAPTER NINE

INDIA THOUGHT SHE'D attended fancy balls before,
but she very quickly realised that nothing within
her experience prepared her for something of
this magnitude. The modern façade of the high-
rise was exactly that—a façade—behind which a
centuries-old building stood wrapped in a lush,
overgrown courtyard, the gardens of which had
been strung with fairy lights overhead, and, on
the ground, covered in a delicate carpet of tea
lights, so it looked like something out of *A Mid-
summer Night's Dream*. An orchestra played
and, while their song was unified, they stood
throughout the gardens: a cluster of three violin-
ists here, a pianist there, an ensemble of flutists
and a clutch of harpists, so that the delightfully ethereal music wafted and breezed on the
wind—both all-consuming and delicate at the
same time. The details took on a new importance
to India as a sort of coping mechanism, and she
immediately understood why Khalil had pre-

sumed their kiss at the bar in New York might have been photographed.

Here, he was the star of the ball, every eye on him at all times—which meant that every eye was also on her. It wasn't simply about attention, but also appraisal, as dozens of women eyed her with barely concealed envy.

So he was considered to be that much of a catch, huh? Well, she could see why, from the outside at least. He was devastatingly handsome, wealthy, powerful, and on the first night they'd met, he'd been charming—if, oh, so arrogant. But he was the last man on earth she would have chosen to marry if it weren't for their situation! She had to remember that. Only, when Khalil offered his arm, she placed hers in the crook of it, and a blade of desire pressed hard to her breast, so she forgot, for a moment, that she wanted to dislike him…

'I'm suddenly regretting the impulse to bring you here,' he muttered *sotto voce,* so her eyes skittled to his.

'Oh?' Her lips, painted red for the occasion, formed a perfect 'O' and his eyes dropped to them with obvious desire.

He swore softly, drawing her close. 'We won't stay long. It's only a matter of being seen together, then we can leave.'

'What if I'm having fun?'

'I promise you will have more fun alone with me.'

She smiled, and, despite the tangle of emotions pulling at her, surrendered to the sheer sensuality of being near him, of his words, and the power that came from knowing how much he wanted her. It was—for that moment—enough.

'We'll see,' she teased, and he laughed, a soft, throaty noise that made her ache to turn on her heel and slide right back into his car, to leave the crowds behind and be alone with this man. All night, just the two of them…

He caught her hand and lifted it to his lips, kissing the back of it as though he couldn't help himself. Flashes went off—not the paparazzi lenses that had snapped them outside, but the flashlights of phones every guest at the event carried.

'In New York, that would be considered very bad etiquette,' she said under her breath.

'The kiss, or the photos.'

'Both.' She slid him a sidelong glance. 'But I meant the photos.'

'Here too,' he agreed. 'Under ordinary circumstances, but you are the first woman I have been seen with publicly since my engagement ended, so it is natural that your appearance has sparked a flurry of fascination.'

India stared at him, his words not making sense at first. 'I'm sorry, did you just say…you were engaged?'

'Was, yes.'

'What? When? To whom?'

He lifted a brow at her numerous questions. 'Our engagement ended six months ago. It was a mistake.' His voice was stony suddenly, as though he were pushing her away physically. 'And this is not the place to discuss it.'

'Six months ago? So the night we met, it had only been four months—or just over three and a half, in fact,' she clarified, nodding slowly.

'So?'

So, she was a rebound girl. That night had been meaningless to him, even before Ethan had informed him of what he believed India to be. Until that moment, she hadn't realised how hard she'd been clinging onto the spark of what they'd shared, as though it stood in a little box outside normal time, just him and her and a connection that had formed spontaneously and urgently, that had actually meant something.

But it had been nothing. A chance to push his ex-fiancée from his mind, nothing more.

'Dance with me,' he murmured.

'Now?'

'Why not?'

'Because no one else is dancing.'

'We want the world to see us together, do we not?'

'I think your kiss accomplished that.'

He laughed, softly drawing her into his arms, the moonlight above cutting a pale silver swathe through the garden, so her dress sparkled like fairy dust.

'It was barely a kiss,' he reminded her. 'Just a chaste sign of affection.'

'Nonetheless, it will be all over Twitter by now.'

'Perhaps.' He shrugged, beginning to move in time to the music, his body's rhythm captivating hers, so she was dancing along with him even before she realised it. His eyes were the most fascinating shade of brown, and she found her gaze drawn to them, her mind solely occupied in the cataloguing of the flecks of gold. It was tempting to relax into the moment completely, but there was danger in letting down her guard with Khalil, so she forced her brain to keep working, her mind focussed.

'Why did you break up?'

He stiffened, his movements stopping for a moment, earning India's fascination. But at least he didn't ignore the question.

'It would never have worked.'

'That tells me precisely nothing.'

'As I intended.'

India considered that. 'Why? Is it a secret?'

'It is something I prefer not to think about, let alone discuss. And it is part of a past that doesn't affect us—nothing good can come of bringing it out into the open.'

It was India's turn to miss a step, so Khalil's arm tightened around her waist, offering necessary support.

'I believe most things benefit from being brought into the open, in fact.'

'Then let's talk about you,' he quietly cajoled, his words just a whisper in her ear. To anyone looking, they would have seemed like a couple so in love they couldn't stand to have any distance between them whatsoever, but for India, their proximity was a convenient necessity—only at this distance could they speak so frankly without risk of being overheard.

'My response hasn't changed since the first night we met, you know. My life story isn't particularly interesting.'

'Let me be the judge of that.'

'Fine,' she sighed. After all, they were getting married. Of course they should spend time talking, getting to know one another better. Except, India had the strangest feeling that she already knew Khalil, even when there were clearly still so many secrets in his past. 'What would you like to know?'

His response was lightning fast. 'How did someone like you end up doing what you do?'

'A woman like me?' His hand lifted to the flesh at the top of her back, his fingers trilling over her spine slowly, so every cell in her body began to quiver with awareness.

'You are smart, India. You are clever, too, and yet because you are beautiful, you took a job that trades solely on your looks. Why?'

'That's a mischaracterisation, for a start. Making conversation with strangers from varied walks of life is not easy,' she responded with a tilt of her head.

He swayed her sideways, and though there was a crowd of people at the event, she was conscious only of Khalil; his overwhelming charisma absorbed her completely.

'For you, I think it would be.'

'Why do you say that?'

'For the reasons I enumerated already. You are smart and clever.'

Pleasure spread through her, the compliment disproportionately pleasing. She had to remind herself that tiny compliments from Khalil did nothing to erase his enormous insult.

'Thank you,' she murmured, her fingers toy-ing with the hair at his nape on autopilot, so she wasn't even aware she was doing it.

'Who were you going to marry?'

He lifted a brow. 'I thought we agreed not to discuss my ex-fiancée,' he said with quiet determination.

'No, you decreed that we wouldn't discuss her, and because you are used to saying one thing and having it be obeyed, you think that counts as "agreement",' she said calmly, unaware of the way his lips curved in a quick, appreciative smile that he flattened almost immediately. 'But I didn't mean her, anyway. You have to marry before your coronation. I presume there was someone else you had decided to propose to, before this…situation…unfolded?'

'No.' He moved his hand lower, down her spine, to the curve just above her bottom, his fingers splayed wide, holding her close to him so she was aware of his strength and hardness, so that she was aware of all of him. 'There was a shortlist.'

India couldn't help smiling at that, but it was a sad smile, pricked with remorse. 'I see,' she murmured. 'No wonder you're so…'

'So?' he prompted.

'Arrogant.' She lifted her shoulder unapologetically. 'You have a queue of women desperate to marry you. It wouldn't even occur to you that some women don't value marriage to you as the highest prize imaginable.'

'On the contrary,' he responded, and she couldn't tell if he was amused or annoyed. 'You made it very clear that this marriage is the last thing you want.'

'I feel sorry for the women who were hoping you'd turn to them,' she said. 'They'll be heart-broken.'

'I'm sure they'll get over it.'

Silently, India disagreed. If she had loved Khalil, and thought he might want to marry her, she would have had a hard time moving on. He was incomparable. But she didn't say that to him—his ego didn't need any more stroking. His certainty spoke more of his belief that women were fickle and unfeeling. As though he couldn't comprehend true, unfaltering love. Why? What had happened to him? Was it because of his ex-fiancée?

'As for being arrogant,' he said, 'I think that has more to do with how I was raised than anything else.'

Curiosity had her gaze sharpening. 'And how were you raised?'

'With the certainty that I would be master of all I survey.' He said it in a jocular tone, yet India detected a hint of something beneath the surface.

'Specifics, please,' she murmured.

'What would you like to know?'

She cast about for one of the many questions that were swimming through her. 'Well, did you live at the palace, even as a boy? Or did your parents have somewhere a little less…intimidating… when you were younger?'

'The palace has always been my home.'

'So your parents live there now?'

'They do.'

'Where?'

'In the East Wing.'

'Of course.' She narrowly avoided rolling her eyes. 'So you see them often?'

'I see them as infrequently as you likely see your parents.'

Her step faltered, and her hand on his hip dug in a little, as though grabbing hold of something tangible. 'My parents are dead.' She offered a tight smile to put him at ease, as most people would feel regret at having made such a *faux pas*. Her heart ached, as always, because she missed her parents so much it was like a physical injury.

'When?'

Most people would also choose to sidestep the issue, but not Khalil. His insatiable need for answers overrode everything. And yet, despite her first reaction, India realised she wasn't upset to discuss her parents with him. If anything, she felt that talking about them now was a way of bringing them into her life. 'A little over a year ago. It was a car accident,' she forestalled his next question. 'They died immediately.'

'I'm very sorry to hear it. Were you close?'

India stopped dancing, pain lancing her now. 'Very.' Her voice was croaky; she looked away. 'I think we've done what we needed to here, don't you?'

But a muscle jerked low in his jaw and he didn't release her. 'My cousin Astrid lost her parents,' he said, stroking her back, the comforting touch almost kind, except 'kind' wasn't a word she would use to describe Khalil. 'She was much younger, so it is not really a comparison—she never really knew them actually, so it's more the idea of them she misses. It's a pain that doesn't seem to get easier.'

'No.' India nodded gently. 'It doesn't. At least, not in my experience.' She found herself pressing her cheek to his chest. Not looking at him made it easier to talk. 'My mother had actually been sick for a couple of years before the accident. Cancer. It was aggressive, so we were prepared for the worst. Though she'd been granted special permission to take a drug that wasn't approved for treatment, and it was helping. I thought I'd made my peace with losing her, but I hadn't. It was an awful time in my life.'

He kissed the top of her head and butterflies

spread inside her, buzzing through her limbs. It was just an act, he was playing a part, but the effect of his attention was very, very real. She lifted her face to his, and when their eyes locked, it was as though nothing existed beyond them. Their past no longer mattered. Except it *did*, her brain interjected swiftly. Nothing about what she'd just revealed to Khalil changed a damned thing.

'Before my mother married my stepfather, we were alone, and I was lonely. Then, overnight, I had a father—a real one, who truly cared about me—and soon enough, a little brother for me to dote on.' Her smile was ethereal, so Khalil's gaze dropped to her lips.

'You have a brother?'

'Yes. I was very lucky. I had, for a while, the most perfect family.' She pulled her lips to the side, lost in thought.

He ran a finger over her cheek, saying nothing, promising nothing. What could he offer, anyway? He'd been completely honest with her. Love would have no part in their marriage, and it was love that had made her family perfect. Love between her mother and stepfather, and both parents and children. They had been a team. She and Khalil would never be that, but with luck, they could love their children enough to compensate. She had to cling to that hope because she had always sworn she would never get married unless she could find someone who made her as deliriously happy as her stepfather had her mother.

'Excuse me, Your Highness.' A servant appeared as if from nowhere. 'The Prime Minister is asking for you.'

A scowl—unmistakable and fierce—crossed Khalil's face. 'I'm sure he can wait until tomorrow.'

'He says it's important.'

'It's fine.' India took a step back, the appearance of the servant offering her a reprieve from their play-acting.

Khalil's frustration was palpable, though, and she understood it: he didn't like to be interrupted. 'Tell him I'll be a moment. There's someone I'd like to introduce India to first.'

Astrid was a very kind and thoughtful companion. She spoke flawless English, courtesy of having attended university in London, and while beautiful and immaculately dressed, she was also friendly enough to set India completely at ease.

'It's a whirlwind, isn't it?' Astrid laughed as India's eyes skimmed the crowd, mesmerised by the beautiful dresses and elegant guests.

'It really is. I don't know if I've ever seen anything so beautiful.'

'Then you should ask my cousin to take you to

see the fireflies of the Athani Caves. They will captivate you more than you can imagine.'

'I've never seen a firefly.'

'At Athani, you will see thousands. They are blinding in their beauty.'

'I'm sure they are,' India said, almost wistfully, because she suspected Khalil would have little interest in taking her to some caves to see the insect life. After all, what would the point be? There was no chance of being photographed to substantiate their relationship somewhere so remote, and that was what this dating charade was all about—giving his people a chance to adjust to the idea of his girlfriend before she became his wife.

'Khal seemed to enjoy dancing with you. It's nice to see him happy again,' Astrid said with a gentle smile, flagging down a passing waiter. 'Would you like a champagne?'

'Just a juice would be great, thanks.'

Astrid gave the order to the waiter then turned her attention back to India.

'Was he ever unhappy?' India asked, feeling a hint of guilt for prying. After all, if Khalil didn't want to discuss his break-up then she shouldn't try to extort information from his cousin.

'Has he told you about Fatima?'

India hazarded a guess that this must be the

name of his fiancée. 'His fiancée,' she said with a soft nod. 'He's mentioned her, in passing.'

'I see.' Astrid's manner changed, her expression growing more circumspect. 'It was a messy break-up. He wasn't himself afterwards. I was worried he might suffer the effects of her… choices…for a long time. But you seem to have brought him back to life, India, and for that I am most grateful.'

The waiter returned with two glasses of juice. India thanked him in his own language, having been listening to tutorials since arriving. After all, her children would speak this as their native tongue, so naturally she needed to learn the language also.

As their conversation moved on, India found herself dwelling on Astrid's final remark, surprised to realise how much she wished that were true—that she could have been responsible for bringing Khalil back to life. The truth was, though, he was still as cold as ever before; he was simply acting out a role tonight.

CHAPTER TEN

'I LIKED ASTRID very much.'

'You want to talk about my cousin, *now*?' he drawled, propping up on one elbow, feathering his fingers over her breast so she sucked in an uneven breath. And yet she smiled, and the dawn light filtering into his bedroom washed over India, bathing her in almost pure gold so her hair shimmered and her eyes shone.

'She's sweet,' India said. 'And funny.'

'Correct on both counts. She must have liked you too, because usually she is reserved with people she doesn't know well.'

'She wasn't at all reserved with me.'

'As I said, she must like you.'

India felt immeasurably pleased by that.

'She came to the palace when she was only a few months old; she is like my annoying younger sister,' he said with a grin that showed he wasn't serious. India thought of Jackson, and how much their sibling relationship had shaped her life. Even now, every decision she made was with him in mind. 'Her life has not been easy,' he continued quietly, his brows knitting together as he concentrated on his thoughts. 'She was bullied as a little girl, by some children at her school. My parents didn't realise at first. It was only after I read Astrid's diary—I was twelve—' he defended, 'that I understood what was going on.'

'Astrid was bullied?'

'She was different,' he said. 'She was royal, an orphan, and naturally quite shy. It was easy for her to be picked on.'

Indignation fired in India's belly. 'Children can be so horrible,' she said with anger.

'Yes.'

'What happened? Did she change schools?'

'No.' His lips curved into something like a grimace. 'I started taking her to school, walking her to class. I suppose I saw myself as her bodyguard. There was one particularly cruel little girl who used to call her—the equivalent in English would be "loner"—and I...had a word with her, about the wisdom of continuing to taunt Astrid in this manner.'

'You defended her,' India said, her heart fluttering at this show of character. It didn't surprise her—she could tell that Khalil had a form of moralism that was black and white—and yet imagining him as a young boy storming into Astrid's school to look out for her made India's chest swell.

'Until she learned to defend herself. And she did. Astrid grew strong at school, because she had to be.'

'You said she was married, but I noticed last night she wasn't wearing a wedding ring.'

'No.' His lips were grim and now when he looked at India, she had the sense he was holding something back.

'What happened?'

'She married the wrong man.' He hesitated a moment, an uncharacteristic pause. 'Her husband was charming at first. We were friends, I introduced them, so she trusted him from the start. It was a whirlwind romance, and Astrid fell in love hard and fast. They married months after meeting, but it was a disaster. Astrid fell pregnant quickly, and he began screwing around behind her back, sleeping with half of Khatrain's elite.'

Indignation burst through her. 'That's terrible!'

'So you can see why, when I had a chance to take something precious from him, I did not hesitate,' he murmured, his finger tracing an invisible circle over her shoulder, his eyes holding hers meaningfully.

It took India a moment to understand, and then realisation slammed into her like a stack of bricks. 'Are you saying Ethan Graves is her ex-husband?'

'Yes.'

India flopped onto her back, her brain exploding, her mind needing to process that without the intensity of his watchful gaze. 'And that's why you threw it in his face that you were taking me home,' she said with a quiet nod, her brain still making connections. 'Is it *why* you took me home?' she asked, angling her face back to his. His jaw was square in his face, his eyes darkened by emotions she couldn't comprehend.

'It was a part of it.' Hurt split her heart in two.

'I see,' she said unevenly, pushing back the sheet and standing, her pulse in overdrive. She had come to his room straight from the ball, and her gown was the only item of clothing she possessed here. She lifted it off the floor, shaking it so the skirt fell straight and she could step into it more easily.

'What are you doing?'

'Getting dressed.'

'Why?'

'Because it doesn't seem appropriate to walk through the palace in just my underwear.'

'Then stay here.'

'No.'

'Why not?'

'Damn it, stop interrogating me. Isn't it obvious? Do you really need to ask?'

'You are angry. For what reason?'

She bit down on her lip, shaking her head with impatience. They were so disconnected, her emotions nowhere near in tune with his.

'Because,' she blurted out, staring up at the ceiling. 'You—' but she clutched the rest of that close to her chest, something holding her back from answering him too honestly. 'It doesn't matter. I just want to be alone.' She yanked the dress on, pulling her hair over one shoulder so that the zip at the back wouldn't get caught. She could only get it halfway up in her anger, but she didn't care.

'Allow me.' His gravelled offer was the last thing she expected.

She shook her head. 'No. I don't want you to touch me right now.'

He lifted a sceptical brow, which only made her fury grow. She strode towards the door, hands balled into little fists.

His harsh laugh erupted through the room. 'Stop.'

She didn't.

She heard the rustle of sheets and his feet on the floor behind her, and as she reached the door he was there too, his palm pressing down on it. 'Don't run away from me.'

'Don't tell me what to do.' She whirled around to face him.

'Then stop acting like a child and tell me why you are upset.'

'You just admitted you used me to hurt Astrid's ex-husband, and you actually have to ask why that bothers me?'

He frowned at her, still clearly not comprehending.

'Forget about it,' she snapped. 'I don't want to discuss this. I knew you were callous and heartless when I first arrived here, I don't know why I let myself start to think that you were different.'

'Talk to me,' he demanded, his hand on the door forming a sort of barrier, enclosing India. She stared at a point beyond his shoulder.

'You have said worse things to me than anyone in my life. You have hurt me, you have demeaned me, and you have insulted me.' She looked at him square in the face now and had the satisfaction of seeing something fleck in the depths of his eyes. But was it guilt? Remorse? 'But that night…' She shook her head sadly. 'That night was…before all this. I know our babies weren't conceived out of love, but I had been telling myself they were at least conceived out of intense attraction, and some kind of spontaneous affection. I *liked* you, Khalil. I went home with you because I really, really liked you. I actually—'

She swallowed back the words but he leaned closer, his voice gravelled. 'You actually what?'

Forcing her eyes to meet his, she spoke honestly. 'It was my birthday that night. It was my first birthday since losing my parents and I was struggling. Then I met you and everything just lit up. I actually joked to myself that you were some kind of gift from me to me.' She rolled her eyes at the stupidity of the very idea. 'I didn't care that you were royal; I just wanted to be with you.' Emotions clogged her throat. 'I wasn't thinking about anything that night except for that. Liking you. But you were just using me for revenge.'

Her skin blanched, her eyes closing. 'And then you had the nerve to accuse *me* of being mercenary? You have been hanging that over my head since I got here, as though I was the one who turned that night into something sinister and cynical, but you're the one who chose to seduce me because of who I was with. You're the one who threw it in Ethan's face, even when we'd agreed I would make up an excuse, lie to him, to avoid insulting him. You did that because you wanted to hurt him, and instead, it hurt me. I lost my job because of what you did, and you didn't even care. You have all this, you wouldn't have any idea what it's like to need to work, to go from pay cheque to pay cheque. And all for what? So you could avenge Astrid? Do you think that's what she would have wanted? If she knew what you did, do you think she'd be proud of you?'

'She was devastated by their marriage breakdown.'

'As I am devastated by our marriage agreement,' India whispered. 'But I guess that doesn't matter. I'm no one to you, and never will be, right?'

He stared at the closed door for several seconds, her words slicing through him with all the intensity of a fierce sandstorm, and then he wrenched it inwards, striding to catch up with her. Of all the accusations she'd hurled at him, each had merit, but there was one that was pulling at him, so he found it hard to move. It had been her birthday. She'd chosen to spend it with him. It was such a sweet, lonely admission; how could it fail to touch something deep in his chest?

She went quickly, and was a long way down the corridor, yet he could have reached her easily if he'd wanted to. He let her go ahead, his heart pounding as he followed after. Even in anger, she exuded a classic elegance that was impossible not to notice, or admire.

She turned into the corridor that housed three guest suites, passing two guards stationed there as she went. They kept their eyes forward-facing, but as Khalil passed they bowed.

He strode past them without acknowledgement, reaching her door just as she went to close it.

'Wait,' he said gruffly, pressing his forearm against it, holding it ajar.

'Why? Is there anything more to say, Your Highness?'

He hated it when she used his title; it put distance between them, a distance he didn't want. 'Let me in.'

For a moment, he wondered if she was going to refuse—and what he would do if she did! Every bone in his body wanted him to speak with her some more, but he wasn't going to strong-arm his way into her suite if she was determined to keep him out. He stood where he was, something strange gripping his chest, a sense of concern he couldn't comprehend. Even when she stepped back to open the door wider, the worry didn't evaporate.

'Thank you,' he said, pacing into the room and putting his hands on his hips.

'What do you want?' She matched his gesture, hands thrust on hips, eyes glaring through his.

'I noticed you before I saw him,' he said, before he could stop himself—it was something he'd never wanted to reveal to her. And yet, faced with her obvious devastation, and the reasons for it, he knew he couldn't lie to her, even when some form of self-preservation was pushing him to. It would be better if she believed it had all been a ruse to make Ethan sweat, but that wasn't the sum total of why they'd come together.

'I saw you across the room and felt like I'd been smacked in the gut. I wanted you and I swore I'd have you, regardless of who you were with. Seeing it was Ethan was a way to kill two birds with one stone, I suppose. But that's not why I wanted you.'

She didn't respond, but her body was taut, her spine straight, shoulders squared. There was a defensiveness about her that made him ache, and it was all the worse because he'd done this to her. It was late in the day to realise how much he liked seeing her smile.

'Whether you were with Ethan or not, I would have wanted you, India. I would have done everything I could to take you home with me.'

The admission was wrenched from deep inside; he felt as though he was giving away a part of himself he had wanted to keep firmly boxed up.

'It doesn't matter,' she said softly, the words rich with sadness. His gut twisted.

'It clearly *does* matter. You are upset.'

'Yes.' She nodded curtly. 'I am. And a half-hearted explanation that, actually, you *were* kind of attracted to me after all doesn't change the fact that you used me. What other explanation is there for the fact you told him we were going home together?'

'I have already admitted I wanted to take something from him, something of value. I had no idea then that your date was simply an…arrangement.'

She closed her eyes.

'No, you didn't. You thought we were a couple, and you decided to take me from him. But it was never actually about me. It was about you and Ethan and Astrid.'

'You're not listening to me. I'm saying—belatedly—that I wanted you *before* I knew he was your date.'

'And I'm supposed to be flattered by that?'

'You're supposed to see that you're right—what we shared that night was about you and me, not him. No one else.'

'You waved our leaving together in his face!' she shouted. 'You hate this man. He has shown himself to be the worst of the worst, yes?' she demanded fiercely. 'What he did to Astrid was an abomination, I understand that. But nothing excuses what *you* did to *me*. I didn't ask to be a part of any of this.'

'If my sole purpose was to hurt him, I could have bragged about taking you home and then dropped you back at your place. Spending the night together was unnecessary to finalise that part of my intentions.'

'Come on, Khalil. You're still a red-blooded man. You were hardly going to look a gift horse in the mouth, especially one giving themselves to you so freely.' She paused angrily, shaking her head. 'Not so "freely", of course. You believed there would be a charge at the end of the night.'

'Don't,' he ground out, irritation and impatience and anger all snapping through him. 'I'm trying to say that before Ethan sullied what we shared with his...revelation, I had one of the best nights of my life. Our babies were conceived out of something good. Something that was special to both of us, at the time.'

'But it wasn't.' She shook her head. 'It was brought about by hate. And if you don't believe me, let me show you how I know this to be true.'

His breath exploded from his lungs, angry and fast. His words were being twisted, and he had only himself to blame. Hadn't he intentionally misled her about that night? He had wanted to protect himself, and so he'd misled her as to the true reason he'd taken her home, but it had backfired, spectacularly. He would do anything not to have India feel like this.

'You have told me what Ethan did to Astrid. He is a horrible man, I agree. Despicable, untrustworthy, and mean.'

He dipped his head at her accurate assessment.

'And yet you believed him, about me,' she whispered.

His eyes narrowed as he recognised the devastation on her face.

'He told you I was a prostitute, and it didn't once occur to you to doubt his word.'

Khalil was not used to feeling in the wrong. His arrogance was born, primarily, from the fact he had excellent instincts and used them wisely. Her logic was, however, flawless.

'He sent me the agency listing,' Khalil pointed out, his voice ringing with a certainty he no longer felt. 'It wasn't only his word, but also the evidence.'

'Evidence,' she snarled, crossing her arms hard across her chest. 'That was no evidence. Not of what you're accusing me of, at least. I worked for an escort agency, yes. I went on dates with people who, for whatever reason, needed a companion for the evening. One of my favourite clients was an eighty-two-year-old man whose wife died ten years ago. We would go to the theatre together once a month. Do you think I was having sex with him, too?' She shook her head angrily. 'Only you could take what is a perfectly legitimate job and turn it into something else.'

'I had you investigated, after that night.'

'I know. You spied on me. I remember.'

'I wanted to know if it was true. I hoped—I wanted to believe—'

But she didn't let him finish. 'If you had me investigated then you must know that I do not go home with the men I date.'

'There was no evidence of that,' he said warily. 'But there was plenty of evidence that many of the women who are hired out by Warm Engagements do in fact bed their clients.'

India gasped. 'That's against the rules.'

He stared at her, the response more telling than anything else could be. Light blinded him, and he turned away, so that she wouldn't see on his face the comprehension that was dawning—the realisation that he might have seriously misjudged her this whole time.

'And you didn't know that then,' she reminded him softly, her voice trembling as she returned to the original point with effortless focus. 'The morning after we slept together, you had only Ethan's word and my agency listing to go off. You wouldn't let me explain myself. You wouldn't believe me.'

No, he wouldn't. Because everything she'd said had reminded him of Fatima. He'd been fooled once, badly, and he would never forget what that had cost him. The idea of being duped all over again had made him react harshly—more harshly than he should have.

'You believed that horrible man over me, and I will never forget that. Not ever. Not when we make love. Not when we marry. Not when we become parents.' Tears sparkled on her lashes and he stood perfectly still, because the alternative was to go to her and pull her into his arms, hold her against him and beg her to forgive him. To forgive him? Khalil's compass no longer faced in a recognisable direction. Confusion swamped him. 'I really, really hate you right now, Khalil. Please, just leave me alone.'

CHAPTER ELEVEN

STANDING BESIDE HIM and not speaking was a form of agony, so too their obvious desire to avoid touching. The horse race was well attended, reminding her of news footage she'd seen of Ascot or Australia's Melbourne Cup, well-dressed men and women piling into the racecourse, prepared for a day of fun and adventure.

In other circumstances, India might have enjoyed the day, but the argument she'd had with Khalil—several days ago now—was still festering in the back of her mind. She'd tried to make her peace with what had happened, but the more she thought about it, the angrier she became, the more hurt.

That he would trust someone like Ethan Graves over her!

Hearing him speak about the other man's conduct, she could perfectly understand why Khalil had wanted to hurt him, but to allow her to become collateral damage?

'After the morning's events, I will have to leave you for a time. It's tradition for me to ride a lap of the course.'

She nodded without looking at him. One of the servants who'd helped her dress for today had already explained the procedure. 'Fine.' She didn't look at him.

'India,' he sighed. 'This has to stop.'

She compressed her lips.

'The doctor said you are not supposed to be upset.'

She fidgeted her fingers at her sides. 'I'm fine.'

'You have not been fine for days.'

It was true. They'd seen each other multiple times and she'd barely spoken to him. She wasn't trying to prolong their argument, only she had no idea what to say. Her heart was in tatters, her mind furious. She hadn't realised how desperately she'd been clinging to the idea that their first night together had been about something else, something completely separate from all of this.

She'd been wrong.

She'd been a pawn to him, a dispensable, worthless tool to inflict pain on a man who didn't even deserve his consideration.

It was impossible to forgive.

'Do you blame me?' she asked, looking up at him finally.

He swallowed hard. 'No.' Surprise stirred in her eyes. 'I don't blame you at all, India.'

She looked away quickly, emotions rioting. They were just words, but they moved through her in a way that was terrifying, so she needed to remember why she was so angry with him, why this was all such a disaster.

His fingers curled around her cheek, turning her to face him. 'We can leave.'

'We *can't* leave,' she demurred. 'We are in a royal box with cameras trained on us. You have to ride your lap of honour or whatever. We're stuck.' And she didn't just mean here, at this fancy horse race. They were stuck in every sense of the word, trapped by one night, for the rest of their lives.

He shook his head. 'We can leave.'

She didn't respond this time. Aware of the cameras, she lifted her hand to his, removing it from her cheek. To the outside world, it was a moment of shared affection, but for India, she simply needed him to stop touching her. She felt too much, even then, swaying towards him as though there were an inevitability to their being together, when that wasn't—couldn't be—true.

'And then what, Khalil?' She let the words fall between them, rock boulders into choppy water. 'Tomorrow there'll be another event, and another the day after that. This is my life now.' She swallowed hard, but a lump in her throat made it almost impossible to breathe. 'There's no sense trying to run away from it.'

He wanted to ride his horse as he did in the desert. He wanted to lean low to the stallion's mane and whisper words of urgency, to kick his side three times, fast, so that the beast took flight, carrying him as though he would make for the horizon at any moment. He wanted to ride far away from here, and this. But not all of this. His eyes sought her without his permission, landing on the royal box and scanning the seats until he found her. She was still standing, as they'd been together, her eyes trained on him. Even at this distance, he could feel her tension, her stress and strain.

There's no sense trying to run away from it.

He turned the corner, so his back was to her now, and he resisted—just—a desire to cast a glance over his shoulder.

She was right. They couldn't run away. Though the desert beckoned him, there were no answers there. It was no longer an escape path for him. Khalil's place was here, with her. They were having children together, and she had agreed to marry him. In a matter of months, he would be crowned Sheikh of Khatrain and all the responsibilities of ruling this great country would fall to him.

They would live together as man and wife and they would need to forge a path that didn't involve so much recrimination.

He couldn't hurt her again.

He sat up straighter, the clarity almost blinding. He hated himself for what he'd done to her. More clarity. He didn't want her to feel as she did now. He wanted to make her happy. He wanted a fresh start.

Everything exploded inside him at once, so now, with renewed purpose, he did speed his horse up, dismounting as soon as he'd finished the lap. He lifted one arm into the air in a gesture of acknowledgement; the crowd roared their applause. He barely heard it. He took the steps two at a time, pushing past his security into the private enclosure, taking the next staircase until he reached the royal box.

It was empty.

'Are you better?'

He stormed into her room without so much as knocking, but India had expected that. She turned to face him slowly, her face pale.

'India?' His voice was tortured. 'Are you okay? Is it the babies?'

A sense of guilt formed in her gut. It hadn't even occurred to her that he'd be genuinely concerned, nor that he'd think the note she'd left pleading 'a headache' might indicate anything more severe.

'I'm fine,' she said with a shake of her head.

'"Fine" again?' he demanded, crossing to her and pressing his palm to her forehead. She pulled away, but he put a hand on her hip, holding her close. 'What is it? Do you need the doctor?'

She shook her head. 'It was just a headache. From the heat, I think. I feel better now. I've had some water and rested a little.'

His eyes scanned her face with care. 'I'm glad to hear it.'

She swallowed, looking away from him. 'You shouldn't have come back early. I didn't mean to spoil your fun.'

'I wanted to check on you,' he explained slowly, as if lost in thought.

'It wasn't necessary.'

He sighed with exasperation. 'Actually, it is perfectly necessary. We need to talk.'

Her eyes swept shut on a wave of dread. 'What about?'

'This marriage.'

She felt as though she were approaching a precipice with no idea if she were to be thrown off it or not. 'What about it?'

'This won't work.'

Her heart stammered almost to a stop.

'I don't want to see you like this. I don't want to make you miserable. You don't deserve this.'

Her eyes flared wide. 'Are you…saying…you don't want to get married?'

He stared at her, silent, shocked. 'No,' he said, firmly. 'I don't mean that.'

She frowned. 'So, what?'

'The fact that you're pregnant means we must marry. There's no other way. I can't order the twins into the line of succession if they're born out of marriage. We've discussed that.'

'Then I don't understand what you're saying now.'

'I want this marriage to work. More than that, I don't want to fight with you. It has to stop. Neither of us can live like this.'

Her heart stammered, because he was right, but it was still so clear that he thought the worst of her. Even after all that she'd said to him, pleading with him to accept her version of events, he still didn't. And he never would.

'I want us to start over. I want us to focus on the good between us—the babies we are to raise—and nothing else. I want us to remember that there is chemistry here and that we can make whatever future we want for ourselves. But most of all, I don't want to see you sad and miserable and to know that I am the cause of that.'

His words, on some level, were important—

she needed to hear them. But at the same time, they were just a further reminder of how false all this was.

'I want you to be happy.'

Her smile was weak. 'That's very kind of you.'

'Damn it, it's not kind. I have been the exact opposite of kind, please don't say otherwise. But I do want to fix this, India, and I have every intention of succeeding.'

Her stomach squeezed. 'Why?'

Silence fell, thudding around them, and finally, he spoke. 'Our children deserve that we at least try, don't they?'

'But how do we do that? After everything that's gone between us?'

'Have dinner with me tonight.'

'We have an event.'

'We'll skip it. It doesn't matter. This is more important.'

Something fluttered in her chest. But hope refused to settle. 'I don't think a dinner is going to solve this.' Whatever good he claimed lay between them, there was bad, too, and it stretched unendingly.

'Isn't it worth, at least, the attempt?'

Her eyes probed his, her heart frozen in her chest, her nerves firing disjointedly. Was he right? Did they owe it to their children to at least attempt to form a truce of sorts?

'Where?' she said, after a beat.

Satisfaction arranged his features. 'Leave the details to me. I'll meet you here, at eight.'

In the end, he sent a servant instead, a man dressed in a suit who greeted India one minute after the hour. India wore a simple dress—the same one she'd brought with her from America—and teamed it with a pair of sandals. She'd left her hair out, flowing loose down her back in voluminous waves. The servant took her away from the guest suites and through the palace, a circuitous route that she would have no hope of backtracking if she were forced to make her own way. Eventually, they emerged into a courtyard, and, beyond it, a large open space that housed a gleaming black helicopter.

Khalil stood beside it, his arms crossed, his eyes watchful.

She was a mix of nerves and anticipation, but it was anticipation that was at the fore as she moved towards the vehicle, the servant forgotten, nothing penetrating her mind now but this man and her awareness of him.

'Good evening, India.'

His voice wrapped around her, warmer than the night air. 'Khalil,' she responded in kind, dipping her head in a nod, earning a smile from him.

'After you.' He gestured to the rear doors of the helicopter.

She hesitated.

'Is there a problem?'

She sent him a sidelong glance. 'Well, I've never been in one before,' she said with a slight laugh.

'There's a first time for everything.'

He was right, and their marriage would be like this too. It would be a first for them both, and they would need to learn a lot as they went. Screwing up her courage, she stepped into the helicopter. And though she was braced for it to be luxurious, the sheer decadence of the interior nonetheless took her breath away. From the plush white leather seats to the wood grain details, to the bar fridge in the centre that boasted an array of expensive champagne, she felt as though she'd entered the twilight zone.

'Would you like a drink?'

'Mineral water?'

He nodded, indicating that she should take a seat on the long bank of three at the rear of the helicopter. She did so, fastening her seat belt while he retrieved a couple of bottles of water.

A moment after he took the seat beside her, the rotor blades began to spin, and the door was slammed shut by a servant.

She jumped, so he laughed softly. 'Relax,

azeezi.' He leaned closer to her. 'It's perfectly safe.'

'It's probably very normal for you,' she murmured. 'But this is a big deal for me.'

He put his arm along the back of the chair, his fingertips casually brushing her shoulder. 'Try to enjoy the experience.'

As it turned out, her nerves settled as the helicopter lifted into the air. Or perhaps they just became focussed on another element of the night. His fingers moved softly over her skin, sending little sparks and shock waves through her, so that within moments she'd forgotten that they were in the air in a machine that could hardly be described as aerodynamic. A moment later, the view drew her attention, so she shifted, closer to the window, her eyes chasing the incredibly beautiful city, so that Khalil stared at her, his eyes observing every shift on her face, all the fascination and wonder dancing in her features.

The helicopter ride took twenty minutes. They passed the city and tacked further south, before moving inland, covering a vast expanse of desert that finally gave way to a gentle mountain range.

The helicopter set down at the foot of it, and then the doors were opened.

'This is…the middle of nowhere,' she said with an uneven laugh.

'Not quite.'

'Where is it, then?'

'The Athani Mountains.'

She blinked, excitement bursting through her. 'The fireflies?'

'Astrid suggested it.'

India grinned. 'I've never seen them before.'

'She said that too. I thought a new chapter in our relationship required a new experience.'

'Two,' she corrected. 'The helicopter and the fireflies.'

'Even better.' He kissed the back of her hand, his eyes holding hers. 'I want to make this work, India.'

Her heart pounded hard against her ribs, and she nodded. 'I know that.' A sigh whooshed through her, as finally she reconciled herself to this decision. 'I do too.'

It felt more meaningful than when she'd agreed to marry him. That had been logistical, this was more. It was a statement of intent, a promise to make this work, to be good to one another, to find a way to parent their children together that didn't involve navigating a warzone; to be a family.

She slipped her shoes off as she exited the helicopter, transferring them to her other hand, so that it was easier to walk across the cool desert sand. Khalil did likewise, catching her hand in his, lacing their fingers together. She blinked up at him then wished she hadn't, because the moon was shining on him like a spotlight, making him appear larger, and like the only person in her world.

A new start was good, but it was a mistake to get too carried away. This was still essentially a business arrangement. He needed a wife, he needed heirs, and she was pregnant with his twins. She wanted her children to grow up in a family, she wanted his support, and, yes, she needed his financial help. There were reasons for them to enter into this marriage—a marriage neither would even be contemplating if it weren't for the unique circumstances that were playing out.

This wasn't love.

It wasn't special.

It was—

'Oh, wow.' She stopped walking about twenty yards from the entrance to the caves. A swarm of fireflies danced past them, their delicate, ethereal beauty shimmering in the night sky, their little bodies aglow with what looked like embers. 'They're—incredible.'

'Wait for it,' he said, squeezing her hand and drawing her with him, nearer to the caves. Once inside, she saw what he meant. Here, they were everywhere, flying through the tunnels, creating enough light to easily see by. They ignored India and Khalil, exploring the ancient cave walls instead.

'They are spread throughout the kingdom, but this is the most numerous collection. It's the perfect environment for them, the right climate and light, the best food source.' He hadn't relinquished her hand. 'When I was a young boy, it was my favourite thing to do with Astrid. We would come to these caves whenever we could, and watch them fly around. I would try to catch them, but as soon as I did their lights would go dim, as though they were hiding from me. I found it hard to reckon with that, at the time. Admiring them so much I wanted to grab some, to take home with me, but realising that if I did so, I would lose what I had loved.'

'A predicament,' she murmured, imagining him as a child. 'Was there no way to bring some to the palace?'

'Perhaps, but my parents did not encourage it. They reminded me that everything has a place and theirs was here.'

'Your parents sound very wise.'

'They are.'

'You didn't answer me, the other night. I asked how often you see your parents. Are you close to them?'

'I admire them very much.'

She pulled a face. 'That's not exactly an answer.'

He laughed. 'You're right. We are as close as we can be, given the circumstances.'

'What circumstances?'

'I was sent away to school when I was thirteen. I finished high school as a boarder. I missed them, and I changed a lot, in the time I was gone. Afterwards, I went to university, then did a rotation in the military. So for many years there, I hardly saw them. But they're good people, and my father has been an excellent sheikh.'

'Is it tradition for royal children to be sent away?'

'Yes.'

She stopped walking. 'How strong a tradition?'

He grimaced. 'Strong. But not unbreakable. If you do not wish for our children to leave home, then we can arrange an alternative.'

Her heart split. There was so much in that sentence to unnerve her! 'Our children', 'home', and his willingness to be flexible, to accommodate her needs. It was beyond what she'd expected.

'I can't even think about it yet,' she said with a shake of her head. 'It sounds like the last thing I would want. I know that I could never have been separated from my parents at that age.'

'Did you enjoy high school?'

'Yes.' She smiled. 'I had a good group of friends and I loved studying.'

'Was it not something you wanted to pursue, after high school?'

'What?'

'Studying.'

'Oh.' She frowned. 'I did. I went to college for a couple of years.'

It was obviously something he hadn't expected her to say. 'What degree did you undertake?'

'Economics. I dropped out before I could finish.'

'Economics?' His brows shot up.

She laughed. 'What? You don't think it suits me?'

'I just—had no idea.'

'I've always loved economics with a crazy passion.'

'Why?'

'Because it's so visceral. People think it's dry and boring, but they don't understand that it's the framework of our civilisations. Societies are made and shaped by economic policy, all of our programmes for social justice are made possible by the economic forethought of the government. Economic strategies have the power to save lives, enrich whole societies and make fundamental differences to the world—from lowering crime rates in traditionally impoverished areas to expanding healthcare.' Her eyes grew shimmery as she spoke and her cheeks were flushed. 'It's the cornerstone of all societies, it's the underpinning of who we are. I am fascinated by it.'

'Then why did you leave your degree?'

She contemplated not answering, but it was no big secret. Her eyes flicked to his, then away again. 'My mom got sick. I wanted to be closer to her.' She toyed with her fingers. 'And college is expensive.'

'They couldn't afford it?'

'Not really. Not that they ever said that, but I knew what her treatment was costing. I didn't want to risk that she would walk away from her medical needs to keep me in school. The bills were enormous. They needed to dip into our college funds to pay for them.' She lifted her shoulders defensively. 'I came home and helped out around the house, got a job doing secretarial stuff so I could contribute—it wasn't much but even just paying for groceries relieved some of their stress.' India didn't see the way Khalil's expression changed, the look of pity that softened his features. 'And then they died, and there was just Jackson and me, and a mountain of bills—'

'Your brother?'

'Yes.' She smiled as she thought of him. 'He was offered his college placement, right before they died. They were so happy. Medicine's all he's ever wanted to do. Even as a boy, he used to walk around with this little toy med kit, asking to listen to our heartbeats all the time.' Her expression was laced with nostalgia, her eyes sparkling with the warmth of her memories. 'Then Mom got sick and he became even more determined. All he wants to do is help people get better.' She shook her head wistfully. 'I swore I'd do whatever I could to send him through school.'

His eyes closed as he stopped walking. 'And let me guess. His degree will cost one hundred thousand dollars?'

She nodded. 'I should have told you that's what I needed that amount for.'

'You were under no obligation to tell me anything.' He looked away again, so she barely caught his muttered oath. 'But I should have asked.'

'Would it have changed anything?'

He turned to face her, lifting his hand and catching her hair, his eyes on hers. 'It would have helped me understand you better.'

It was such a specific—and low—amount, given her bargaining position. All this time he'd been thinking of her as mercenary, just like Fatima, when she'd given him incontrovertible proof that money was not—and never had been—a driving force for her. Why hadn't he queried that at the time? Why hadn't he asked her why she needed precisely one hundred thousand dollars? Why hadn't he pushed her, when he'd asked about her job, and her reasons for doing what she did?

She hadn't said she 'wanted' one hundred thousand dollars—she'd said she 'needed' it. He'd pushed that aside at the time but now he saw the desperation behind her plea, and the embarrassment she felt at asking for such a paltry sum, and was furious with himself for being so thoughtless. Anger had blinded him and he'd failed to see her predicament. Or had he simply not wanted to see it?

He had taken everything at face value because it had suited him to think the worst of her. It had suited him to see her as another Fatima, to believe she was just the same, driven purely by money, when the more the heard from India, the more he wondered if, actually, everything she did was driven by love.

CHAPTER TWELVE

'TELL ME ABOUT your parents?'

She considered that as he reached up and held back a particularly long and spindly branch of the pomegranate tree.

'Thank you,' she murmured, inhaling the intoxicating fragrance of the citrus grove as they walked, early in the morning, before the sun was too high, through the kitchen gardens. In the distance, a team of servants had scattered, carrying out their work separately but in harmony—some picking fruit, vegetables and herbs for the day's meals, others tending to the garden. Yet despite their presence, India and Khalil were virtually alone. This walk had become a habit of theirs in the week since visiting the wonders of the Athani Caves. Neither had discussed it, but it seemed to happen regardless, and it had become a highlight for India. She relished these opportunities to be alone with Kahlil, to speak with him, to brush her hand against his, to feel his nearness and to realise that they were walking side by side—into a future they would share. It was a different togetherness from what they shared in bed. That was primal and animalistic, driven by an insatiable chemical need to come together. This was slower, more exploratory, as though each were walking a tightrope towards trust and acceptance, trying to find their way to solid ground without falling.

'What would you like to know?' She plucked a lemon blossom from a tree, bringing it to her nose. The aroma was delightfully sweet.

'What did your mother do?'

'She was a teacher,' India said. 'And very passionate about it.'

'And your stepfather?'

'A librarian.'

'Did they meet at school?'

'No, at our local library, actually.' She swished the lemon blossom between her fingertips before passing it to Khalil to appreciate. 'After my father left us, we moved around a bit. Mom struggled with rent, and work—I was only little. It was a very hard time in our lives. I was too young to remember much of it. I know there were times when we were living in a car, eating from food banks.' She shook her head, oblivious to the way Khalil stared at her, his features frozen, hanging on her every word, painting the picture of the life she described. 'Then, one day, we settled, for a while, in Brooklyn. She had a friend from school who lived there—Juanita—who was going to Australia for a year's work. She offered Mom the house on really cheap terms—basically no rent, just the upkeep. It was such a gift—a real opportunity for Mom to claw her way out of poverty. We didn't have much, just a suitcase, and I was an avid reader, even at that age. So Mom would take me to the library, almost every day. And while I was checking out the books—'

'She was checking out the librarian?' he prompted, lifting a thick, dark brow.

'Something like that.' India laughed. 'Dad—I call him "Dad", because he raised me—was so kind. The opposite to my biological father. And he doted on us. He helped Mom get a contract with a local school, even though her work experience had been patchy for a few years. I enrolled in the same school, which meant childcare was easier. And before Juanita came back from Australia, they were married, so we moved in together. They were such a great couple. Anyone who knew them adored them. They were so much fun to be around. Dad was a total dork. He had theme songs for our family, and he'd randomly burst into song when we were out in public, like at the mall. I used to be mortified, but now, that's one of my favourite memories.'

'He sounds unique.'

'Yeah, he was.'

'And your biological father?'

'A total non-event.' She shrugged, the pain in her chest ever-present, even though her birth father didn't deserve that. 'He blew in and out of my life from time to time, when it suited him, but never for long, never with any reliability, and the older I got, the less he knew how to be with me, how to speak to me. Eventually, he stopped coming altogether.'

'And I take it he did not support your mother financially?'

She poked out her tongue. 'Not even a little. He was the worst.'

He stopped walking, a frown on his face. 'India...'

'What is it?'

'I'm very grateful that you came here, to tell me about your pregnancy. I can see how hard it must have been for you, not knowing how I would react, not knowing if I would be like your biological father or your actual father.'

Her heart lifted at his distinction. Despite the fact English was his second language, he had understood the nuance perfectly.

'It *was* hard,' she agreed with a nod, moving towards him and linking their fingers. Sparks flew through her and her heart lifted, but there was always a dark spot within it, a weight that pressed her down to earth. Knowing what he believed her capable of sat like a stone in her gut. She closed off her mind to it, ignoring the threat of an aching pain, wanting to feel only the good and warmth of the morning. 'But worth the risk, I think.'

'I think so too.' His smile blasted light into her world; she returned it without hesitation. 'What about your parents?'

He reached for a flower as they passed by a tree that India didn't recognise. Fragrant with a small blue fruit, the blossoms a pale pink.

'What about my parents?'

'When will you tell them about all this?'

'When you have agreed to marry me.'

She blinked slowly. 'Haven't I agreed?'

'Provisionally.'

India's hand curled over her stomach as she remembered the negotiations they'd had when she'd first arrived in the country. Back then, she'd pushed for a delay, and part of that had included reminding Khalil that the first trimester was a high-risk time in gestation. But the idea of anything happening to the twins made her feel as though she were going to pass out. She couldn't bear it.

'So after twelve weeks,' she said slowly, 'you'll tell them.'

'And we'll announce our marriage.' He nodded. 'If my calculations are correct, that's next week.'

Her cheeks flushed with warmth. 'Yes. Wednesday.'

He nodded, turning away from her, resuming their walk, but at a gentle pace so India found it easy to keep up.

'The wedding will take place Friday evening. Is there anyone you'd like to invite?'

She thought of Jackson, and how strange it would be to marry without him, and yet, at the same time, she didn't want to make a big deal out of what was essentially a convenient arrangement.

'No. No one.'

'Not your brother?'

She glanced at Khalil, wondering how he knew exactly what she was thinking. 'It would feel like lying to him. I don't think I can do that. It's not real.'

'Lying how?'

She sighed. 'We grew up in the same home. We saw what our parents were like, how madly in love, and what a perfect pair. He wants the same things I do—love, happily ever after, you know, the whole deal. I don't know how he'll… when I tell him…'

Khalil frowned. 'You haven't told him?'

'No. We were waiting, remember?'

'But now?'

'Soon.' She nodded. 'I'll have to tell him soon.'

Khalil stared at her as though there were a thousand things he wanted to say, his brows drawn together with obvious non-comprehension, but he let it go, relying on her instincts. She was glad. She didn't want to explain about Jackson, and how she'd always been protective of her younger brother; she didn't want to go into the details of why she didn't want to worry him. She knew he'd be disappointed in her, and for her, and she couldn't bear that.

'Then we will keep the ceremony small: just us, my parents and Astrid.'

'What was your other wedding going to be like?'

A muscle jerked in his jaw, and she could see the topic gave him little pleasure. 'Big.'

'As in, lots of people?'

'Yes.'

She lifted a brow, her tone lightly teasing. 'You're being evasive.'

'Am I?'

She laughed, despite her frustration. 'Obviously. If you don't want to talk about it, just say so; I'll understand.'

He expelled a harsh breath. 'I will talk about anything you wish. But do I need to elaborate?'

The problem was she'd asked simple, 'yes' or

'no' questions. She changed her approach. 'How many people would have come to that wedding?'

'Two thousand.'

She gasped. 'You can't be serious?'

'Yes.'

She bit down on her lip. 'Is it going to be a problem that our wedding is so understated? Perhaps your parents will expect something more substantial?'

'The size of the wedding had nothing to do with my parents.'

She considered that. 'Nor with you?'

'No.'

'So your fiancée wished to invite all those people.'

'Yes.'

'What happened with the two of you? Why did you break up?'

Khalil stopped walking, his hands on his hips as he stared directly ahead. Tension radiated off him in waves. India studied him, knowing she should give him a way 'out', tell him it didn't matter. But curiosity was burning through India, eating her alive.

Finally, he spoke. 'Fatima is very beautiful, sophisticated, clever, and witty. She made me laugh effortlessly with her dry commentary on our mutual acquaintances. My experience with women, before Fatima, was limited to brief affairs. It had never occurred to me that I might fall in love with a woman, because that is simply not how it's done for us. My parents' marriage was arranged by their parents, as was their parents' before them.'

India could barely breathe, and pricks of light filtered through behind her eyes.

'She is also very, very ambitious.'

'And that's a bad thing?'

'No, of course not. But her ambition was solely for wealth and power.'

'Then I suppose it's fortunate she fell in love with a sheikh.'

'She didn't love me.' The words were spoken quietly, but with all the force of a freight train barrelling towards her. 'And she taught me an important lesson about love that I will never forget. Love made me weak. Believing myself in love with her blinded me to all her flaws. I stopped seeing her as a real woman. I idealised her. If I hadn't, I might have anticipated her behaviour. I might have at least known what she was capable of.'

India's lungs were filled with a rush of hot air. She tried to expel it, drawing breath from deep within. He was speaking about another woman but his indictment of love was like a weight on her chest. 'What did she do?'

'What Fatima cared about most in the world was money.' He spat the word with derision, and even though he was speaking about another woman, her tummy swirled. She knew instantly that she'd been tarred with the same brush the morning after they'd slept together—what else could explain the level of his venomous anger? 'My personal wealth is no secret. Separate to the royal income, my family has several businesses and holdings abroad. When it came time to negotiate our marriage contract, she asked for a king's ransom.'

Just as India had.

Heat stung India's ears and she felt nausea spread through her. She pressed a quivering hand to her brow, nodding, silently encouraging him to continue even when a wave of guilt at having asked him for *anything* made it difficult to think straight.

'I had no interest in the negotiations. To me, they were a triviality. Because I was in love.' He spat the word scathingly. 'I left the work to my lawyers; that was a mistake. If I was too emotionally invested, they were not nearly enough. They refused many of her requests, argued over things I would never have cared about. The negotiations stretched on and things between Fatima and me grew tense.'

India pulled her lips to the side in a gesture of deep thought. 'But surely you and she could have talked about it—'

'She would never have showed her hand to me. She wanted me to think our wedding was all about love for her too. And fool that I was, I believed that. If the wedding had happened, she would have had access to anything she wanted. It wasn't necessary for her to do it.'

She didn't need to prompt him. It was obvious that he had disappeared through a time tunnel; he was back in the past, reflecting on the events as they'd happened.

'Negotiations soured. She presumed I knew and had done nothing to salvage them. To punish me, she had an abortion.'

India's lips parted on a noise of shock and horror. 'No.' The word drained out of her.

His face was ashen. 'At least, that's what she said. I don't know if she made it up to wound me. She certainly hadn't told me she was pregnant, but that doesn't mean…' He shook his head, as if that could wipe his grief and worry. 'I have been tormented by guilt. If her claim is true, then the negotiations were responsible for the death of my baby. I couldn't protect my own child.'

But I'll protect these.

A frisson ran down her spine, as understanding shifted in her mind. It was why he'd fought so hard for her to stay in Khatrain, why he needed to see and be near her, to ensure nothing happened during this pregnancy.

'Your fiancée was responsible, no one else.'

'I would have walked over fire to save that baby.'

The sadness in his statement was gut-wrenching. She nodded slowly, tears making her eyes sparkle. 'I know that.' Because that was exactly what he was doing this time around. From the moment he'd heard of her pregnancy he'd done everything he could to draw her into his life, to be sure these babies were cared for. Ultimately, that was what he cared about—making sure history didn't repeat itself, in any way, shape, or form.

'You must hate her.'

He made a sound that was halfway between a gruff laugh and a sigh of disbelief. 'I do. She is the worst of the worst.'

Love had turned to hate; he'd never love again. He'd said that, over and over, and she'd wondered if it was truly possible to live without love, but now it was as if he were whipping her with his words, the very idea tearing something vital and irreplaceable apart inside her, because she understood. She understood *why* he couldn't contemplate loving someone again. He'd loved, he'd trusted, and he'd been burned—the kind of burned from which one didn't recover. What he'd been through was too much. He was broken.

Only, she desperately didn't want him to be.

Her mind was spinning too fast, trying to make sense of a conundrum, but attempting to reach the answer was as difficult as catching soap in the bath. Her brain wouldn't work.

'I was so angry with you that night.' He stopped walking, staring at her. 'After Ethan called me, and said what he did, all I saw was Fatima. I swore I'd never be fooled by a woman again and, in that moment, it was so easy to believe the worst. I was furious—with myself, with you, with the world.'

India's lungs were expanding and contracting without catching air. She felt faint.

'I get it,' she said, slowly, her voice thick. 'I didn't then, but knowing what you went through—'

He lifted a hand, as if to touch her cheek, then dropped it. 'What I went through with Fatima was a nightmare, but it was with Fatima, not you. I should have given you a chance to explain. I should have believed you. God knows I wanted to.'

She looked away, wondering at the mixture of pleasure and pain that was lancing her.

'I have been fighting myself ever since you arrived in Khatrain—for longer, if I'm honest—wanting to believe you, wanting to listen to you, but knowing that listening is a fast track to being lied to.'

It made sense, and, more than that, it showed her how awful his heartbreak must have been, the first time around. She lifted a hand to his chest, sympathy colouring her eyes. 'I'm so sorry for what she did to you.'

'When you told me about your pregnancy, all I could think was that I had to act to protect our baby. I think about that every day, wondering if I missed some vital sign, if I had paid more attention, would things have been different? I don't mean that I wish to have married her, only that for her to have gone to the lengths she did… what did I miss? What could I have done differently?' He lifted his shoulders at the rhetorical question. 'So when you arrived, I swore I would miss *nothing*. I had to keep you here, to know that you were safe and well, that our baby, or babies, as it turned out, were fine. Fear drove me to act in a way I'm not proud of, India.'

His admission pulled at something in her chest. She blinked up at him, her heart exploding with love. She wanted to wipe away his guilt, his worries. She wanted to make him smile.

'From the moment I got to Khatrain we have been in agreement about one thing: that our children are our priority. That's how you've acted. Even when you have made me so mad I wanted to scratch at your eyes, I have always, *always* known that you were fighting for our kids. And

I love that.' Her voice cracked a little as she said the final sentence, her heart begging to be unleashed, to be freed by her admission.

He growled. 'You gave up university to care for your mother, you work a job you are overqualified for to support your brother, and now you make excuses for me. At some point, your heart of gold is going to become a liability.'

'Is it?' She moved closer, so their bodies brushed, and she felt a rush of heat between them, a sensual awareness that she now understood was so rich and urgent because it was driven not just by sex but also by love. 'I think it's going to guide me pretty well, actually.'

He furrowed his brow, not understanding.

'Khalil, listen to me,' she murmured urgently. 'I'm not Fatima. I'm not going to use you, I'm not going to hurt you, I'm never going to lie to you. What I will do, if you'll let me, is be your wife.' She brushed her thumb over his lower lip then pushed onto the tips of her toes, kissing him slowly, savouring the feeling of their mouths dancing together. 'In every way, your real wife.'

'You know that's what I want,' he growled, deepening the kiss, his hands against the small of her back, holding her to him, so stars burst through her and desire ran rampant. He took a step forward, pressing her back against a broad, ancient tree with a wide canopy, so they were shaded from the sun, mostly hidden from view. He found the waistband of her shirt and pushed at it, his fingertips connecting with her bare flesh. A moan was trapped low in her throat, and she succumbed to it, to him and to this perfect moment. But it wasn't simply a moment. It was one moment in a thread of moments, a lifetime of memories they would make together, side by side, just as she'd always wanted.

'I will never get tired of this,' he promised, pushing at her skirt, finding her underpants and guiding them down as he freed himself from his trousers. He lifted her easily, wrapping her legs around his waist and pushing into her, kissing her as he possessed her, as his body moved with hers. She held onto him for dear life, pleasure usurping everything else; every single one of her senses was in overdrive, so the sky, the grass, the warmth, the fragrance of the blossoms that surrounded them, all took on a startling clarity. She dug her nails into his shirt-clad back, her heels interlocked, holding him deep inside until they reached a euphoric, shared release.

It was so perfect, and she knew then that she was right. She loved him. And she had to tell him. That was terrifying, but it was also important—how could she marry him and keep that secret? She'd just promised him she wouldn't lie to him—what was that if not a lie?

'You are incredible.' He kissed her hard, his tongue flicking hers as he lowered her to the ground.

'I need to ask you something.'

He lifted his brow, focussing on straightening his clothes, so he wasn't looking directly at her. 'Right now, you could ask me for all my worldly goods and I'd happily comply.'

She pushed aside his assurance. Wealth, when you were Sheikh Khalil el Abdul, was easy to part with. His heart, on the other hand, was likely under far tighter lock and key.

'We'll see,' she murmured.

'What is it?'

'I'm just wondering how sure you are about the whole love thing.'

'What "whole love thing"?'

'The whole "you'll never love anyone again" thing,' she said, forcing herself to meet his eyes. She saw nothing in his that gave her reassurance.

'I'm very sure,' he said simply, but she knew it was a veneer. He was treading carefully, his hackles rising, his concerns shifting so he was seeking to minimise risk.

But she'd come this far. She couldn't walk away now. 'Because, the thing is, I just wonder if maybe love doesn't have ideas of its own.'

'What exactly do you mean?'

'Don't you think there might be something more here than either of us realised?'

He stared at her without speaking. Only his chest moved, rapidly, so she dropped her eyes to it for a moment, before looking at him once more.

'I think our marriage is based on a pregnancy that was an accident. That's not love.'

She pulled a face, hoping the grimace would hide the waves of uncertainty that were rolling through her. Was he right? Or was she? 'And what about everything that came after? This last month has been so much more than I expected. Getting to know you, spending time together...'

'Yes, it's defied my expectations too.' He spoke gently, almost sympathetically. 'But that's sex, *azeezi*, nothing more.'

Her heart stammered; she shook her head. 'I don't agree.'

'You do not have much experience,' he pointed out softly.

'And you do, but that doesn't make you right and me wrong.'

'In this, it does.' All so gentle! So compassionate! That made her want to break something! She didn't want to be treated like a fragile glass vase.

'So you're saying we can't have great sex and also fall in love?'

'Yes.' He nodded his head to underscore his verbal response.

'Are the two mutually exclusive?'

'No. But love is out of the question for me.' He lifted a hand to her face, but she jerked away from his touch on autopilot—she couldn't bear the kindness, it made her want to cry, and she wouldn't show her vulnerabilities like that. 'I've been honest with you about this. I have never wanted you to care for me. I should have thought it impossible, after the things I said…'

'Initially, perhaps. I didn't fall in love with you because you're perfect.' She sighed. 'If anything, I fell in love with your imperfections, with the way you fought yourself, fought me, fought for our children. I fell in love with you and I needed you to know that, before we got married. I told you I wouldn't lie to you, so I'm not going to. When I say those vows, I'll mean them.'

'India, no.' His features tightened and he stepped backwards, panic radiating from him. 'Listen to me.' There was a new kind of urgency in his tone now. 'This is impossible. You're mistaking lust for love. I understand that—our chemistry is off the charts, but there's nothing more between us than sex. And one day that will fade, we will no longer want each other like this, and you will forget all about loving me. Trust me, this is fiction, fantasy, not fact.'

If it weren't for the tree at her back, she might have stumbled. His words were so completely the opposite of what she'd expected that she didn't know how to respond to them at first.

'Let me get this straight,' she murmured distractedly. 'You think the only thing we share is sex?'

He compressed his lips, dragging a hand through his hair. 'Obviously it's a huge part of it.'

India sucked in a breath that didn't begin to fill her lungs. 'Did you ever stop to wonder why?'

'No.' He crossed his arms over his chest. 'I get the basics of sexual attraction. I don't need to analyse things further than that.'

She rolled her eyes. 'By your own admission, you've never wanted anyone like you've wanted me. Haven't you stopped to ask yourself why that is? Maybe, just maybe, our chemistry is because of our connection, our compatibility.'

'I wanted you the first night I met you, when I knew nothing about you. That wasn't love, it was desire, plain and simple.'

'And revenge,' she remembered with a shudder.

'No, we've dealt with that. I saw you and wanted you before I even knew you were with Ethan. The revenge thing was just convenient.'

'Not for me,' she pointed out, then shook her head, refusing to be drawn into an argument they'd already had out. 'But that's beside the point now. Since I've arrived here, since we agreed to get married, things have changed between us.

Like you just said, you've seen beyond your first impressions, you've got to know the real me.'

'Yes,' he agreed. 'But again, that is not love.'

That hurt. She blinked away from him, a frown line forming between her brows. 'Can you really say that everything we share is just sex?'

He hesitated and for a moment, she had hope. But then he nodded, once.

'So how come we walk like this together each morning? How come we talk about anything and everything that comes to mind? How come you took me to see the fireflies?'

He ground his teeth together, his eyes pleading with her. 'Again, treating you with decency is not love. If I wanted to atone for the way things started between us, then that should be seen as an attempt to improve our relationship, for the sake of our children, nothing else.'

Her lips parted. 'So all of this is, what? Guilt?'

He expelled a harsh breath. 'I wouldn't have put it so crudely.'

She closed her eyes as pain washed over her. 'I'm not asking you for a declaration of love. I just need to know that you're not so broken by what Fatima did that you will never love. I need to know that you're open to loving me.'

He didn't answer. She opened her eyes, trying to read his face, and understanding nothing.

'And that's what I have been trying to tell you

all along. I'm not open to loving anyone. Nor do I believe it's necessary. As I have said, numerous times, we can have a great marriage without that sort of emotional complication.'

'Because of sex,' she whispered.

'Sex, yes. Children. Shared interests. Respect.'

'But not love?'

'No.'

'Never love,' she repeated, for her own benefit more than his, wrapping her arms around her chest and stepping out of the shade of the tree. It didn't improve her temperature; she felt iced to the core.

'I'm sorry.' His voice was soft, coming from right behind her. 'I should have been clearer.'

'You were plenty clear,' she corrected. 'I just didn't believe you.'

They were silent, staring at each other for several long moments.

'This is the last thing I want,' he said, taking a step towards her. 'I don't want you to be hurt any more. What can I do to fix this?'

Her smile was a ghostly impersonation. 'Nothing. You feel as you feel. I just need to learn to accept it.'

She went to walk away but he caught her wrist, spinning her back to him. 'You'll realise that I'm right soon enough. You'll realise that your love for me is an illusion. And I'll be glad when that day comes.'

She nodded awkwardly, tears filming her eyes as she spun away. She knew he was wrong— she would never stop loving him. But she also knew he'd never return it, and suddenly the future seemed desperately bleak. They were getting married, and she faced the prospect of walking down the aisle towards a groom who would never be able to give her the one thing she'd always known she wanted. Leaving him was not an option. Not because of the babies, not because of sex, but because she did love him, with all her heart, and she would do anything to be with him, even if there was torture in that togetherness, because he'd never love her back.

CHAPTER THIRTEEN

THE FACT THAT their wedding was to be intimate did not, as it turned out, mean her outfit was correspondingly plain. In fact, the wedding dress was utterly magnificent. Made of white silk, the gown was fitted to the waist where it flared in a confection of skirts and tulle. Tiny diamonds were stitched into the hemline, giving it a weight that prevented it from flaring too much. There were also diamonds along the neckline, small at the shoulders and decolletage, then enormous at her cleavage, so India balked at even wearing the thing for fear of what it must have cost. Though the dress's opulence was dwarfed by the tiara she was presented with—the diamond in its centre was the size of a large button, shaped like a teardrop, and it was bracketed on either side by equally flawless, shimmering jewels. The weight of it was significant so a team of servants braided her hair to catch the clips, giving it more support.

She watched with an awe that almost edged out her sadness. But not quite.

Her overarching emotion as she prepared for her wedding day was grief. Grief that her mother wasn't with her, grief that her groom didn't love her, grief that she was marrying for practical reasons rather than the fairy tale she'd been foolish enough to hope for.

But it was enough—it had to be. She couldn't change their situation and if she'd had any doubts about Khalil's feelings, his silence since their conversation had shown her the truth.

Nervousness flared through her as a servant appeared at her door. 'It is time, madam.'

India nodded, apprehension tightening every muscle in her body.

'The ceremony is to take place in the Court Rooms,' the servant said, and India appreciated that she didn't refer to it as a wedding. 'Ceremony' felt far more appropriate. This was a simple formality—the legal binding of a man and woman for the sake of their accidental children's future. The more she thought of it in those businesslike terms, the better. Except it wasn't businesslike. She loved him, and, having admitted that to them both, she was plagued with doubts.

There was the sensible solution—marrying him for the sake of their children. She could easily make herself see the points in favour of this plan. It was right that they should be parents together—that was what they both wanted.

But at the same time, her fragile, aching heart was beating her, begging to be heard. Because marrying someone who didn't love you was guaranteeing disaster, wasn't it? What would her mother—who'd struggled with a small child on her own rather than living in an emotionally abusive and hurtful relationship—say about India's choice? Would she understand that India was doing this for love? Or would she remind India that marriage was an important partnership that demanded work and respect, a lifetime of commitment?

A lifetime!

Her knees wobbled as she stood on the threshold of the Court Rooms, shifting to the side suddenly so she could press her back to the wall and stare up at the ceilings. Inside, her fate awaited her. But it was a fate that would require all of her courage to pursue and, suddenly, India wasn't sure if she was brave enough.

'Calm down, Khal. You look as though you're about to fall over.'

He shifted a sidelong glance at Astrid, catching his parents' disapproving glances from their seats a little way across the room.

'She's late.'

'Yes, well, that is a bridal traditional, at least in America. And this is a very big palace. It is quite possible she's wandering a corridor, looking for us, completely lost…'

'Someone was sent to collect her thirty minutes ago.'

'Then she is simply finishing getting ready. Calm down. She'll be here.' Astrid put a hand on his arm, her eyes warm and comforting— neither emotion did anything to reassure Khalil. 'Believe me, Khal. I have seen the two of you together, and I have spoken to India at length. That woman would walk through the desert at midday for you. She'll be here.'

Khalil was very still; even his heart slowed to a heavy, uncertain thump in his chest. 'What?'

Astrid frowned. 'What do you mean, "what"?'

'Why do you say that about India?'

Astrid's expression was quizzical. 'Because she's in love with you. And gathering by the way you're burning holes in the door, and intermittently shaking your watch to ensure it hasn't stopped working, it's quite clear you feel the same about her.'

Anxiety isn't love.

And he was anxious. He realised now how foolish he'd been to ignore her in the lead-up to the wedding. Except 'ignoring' her wasn't exactly accurate. She'd plagued him, head and heart, every minute of every hour since last he'd seen her. Only he'd resisted going to her. He'd avoided seeing her, even when she had somehow become a part of him anyway. Was it possible she would refuse to marry him after all? And then what would he do?

Whatever it takes to make her happy.

Even if that meant letting her go.

He looked around the room with a growing ache in the pit of his gut.

She wasn't coming.

'Why did you marry Ethan?'

Astrid frowned. 'Why does anyone get married? I loved him.'

'Do you regret that now you know what he's like?'

'How can I? I have Romeo. But, more than that, loving Ethan taught me a lot. It's like your experience with Fatima—you went through hell with her, but it made you all the more equipped to recognise true love when you found it.'

He looked away, his throat feeling thick and textured, as though he had razor blades stuck there.

'Love is a huge leap of faith, Khal. It never comes with a guarantee, you know. But look— how beautiful and serene your bride looks.'

His head whipped around, his eyes pinpointing India immediately as she entered the room.

Astrid was right; she was beautiful, but he knew the woman in question better and he saw much that Astrid had missed.

India was strained. Tired. Exhausted. Stressed. Scared. *Terrified*. She also looked completely and utterly…alone.

It was wrong for India to be walking down the aisle like this. Someone should have her arm. Her brother should be here.

It would feel like lying to him.

It's not real.

His heart slammed into his ribs and he stepped forward, instincts stirring to supersede anything else. Everything about this was wrong…

'Excuse me a moment.' He was conscious of his parents' attention on him as he strode down the aisle, aware when his father stood, but Khalil didn't stop. He walked quickly towards India as though she were her own gravitational pull, and he powerless to resist it.

India's stomach was in knots. Her panic attack had receded, but she was still light-headed and uncertain, the enormity of what she was about to do cascading through her like a tsunami. It wasn't helped by Khalil's approach. Was this some custom she hadn't heard of? Was the groom supposed to meet her?

His eyes seemed to lance hers and the intensity in their depths had her steps faltering.

'Is something the matter?' she whispered, when he was right in front of her.

'Yes.' He reached out, touched her hands lightly then immediately withdrew again, angling his face away, his gaze deliberately averted, as though he couldn't bear to look at her. Was the idea of this marriage so terrible to him?

'We need to speak.'

Her heart tripped into her throat. Only minutes ago she'd balked at the idea of marrying him, but now that she stood on the cliff-face of not doing so, she was awash with remorse. It took the spectre of losing him—this—to know without a doubt what she really wanted, regardless of the pain she knew would follow. Some pain was worth enduring.

But what if that wasn't the case for him? What if nothing about this marriage made it worthwhile after all? It was patently obvious that he was having doubts.

'What is the meaning of this?'

His father's voice was booming, a noise that resonated through the room. Khalil reached for her hand now, interlacing their fingers.

India closed her eyes as something like a sense of completion wove through her.

Guard against it. It's not real. Nothing about this is real. He doesn't love you.

'A moment.' Khal responded in the same voice, terser though, as though tension were overtaking him.

'Come with me.' He drew her with him, through a row of seats towards a door at the side of the room, carved from dark, heavy wood. He pushed on it and it creaked a little as it opened to reveal a room that was smaller in size, but no less sumptuous. This had a large red carpet square in the centre, and the furnishings around the room were gold. There was only one window, but it was large and pushed out from the walls, creating a seating area with a view of the rose garden.

He dropped her hand as soon as they entered, then swept deeper into the centre, his back to her, hands on hips. Her heart dropped into her toes. It was clear that whatever he wanted to discuss was negative.

'Khalil,' she murmured, her voice throaty. 'Why don't you just say it?'

He was silent, but slowly, oh so slowly, he pivoted, his eyes unreadable as they locked to hers.

'I mean it. Whatever you're thinking, whatever it is, just say it. I'd rather hear the truth than stand here not knowing.' But she did know. She could see the intent in his expression and was simply waiting for the executioner's axe to fall.

His eyes narrowed, his expression carefully muted of feeling. 'This wedding is a mistake. We cannot marry.'

She'd feared this was coming, but hearing the words shattered a part of her. 'Because I love you?'

'Because you're miserable,' he responded, dragging a hand through his hair. 'Because despite my best intentions I will never be able to make you happy—and I promised that I would try. But I can't. You love me, and I can't give you that. There is no happy ending here for you. You're already miserable—marrying me is only going to make you feel a thousand times worse. We can't do it.'

His words swirled around her, wrapping her into knots, so she didn't know which way was up. 'I'm not miserable,' she contradicted quietly.

'You are. I can see it in your eyes. Marrying you was a simple equation when I didn't know you. Then you were just a woman I'd slept with.' He frowned, a line forming between his brows. 'No, you were never just that to me. I don't know what I'm saying. It was easier when I still thought you capable of—'

'When you didn't care about my feelings,' she said with a tight lift of her lips.

'Yes.' He was arrogant enough to cross his arms over his chest and stare at her unapologetically, but a moment later he grimaced, shaking his head. 'What a monumental ass that makes me. As though I had any right to dictate this decision to you.'

'You didn't dictate, you persuaded.'

'I persuaded by employing threats. That is no different from dictating. If I had given you a true choice, would you have made this one, India?' He didn't wait for her to respond. 'Of course you wouldn't.' The words were grim, and it was obvious that he was angry with himself.

'You don't know that.' She paced slowly towards him, but then changed direction, moving across the room instead. Space was needed. 'I have always known I wanted a family.'

'A true family,' he interrupted gruffly, shaking his head. 'A husband who loves you, children who were created out of that love. Not this.'

Her heart stammered. 'I do love you. So far as I'm concerned, our children are born of love, even if it's not mutual.'

'That's not a good enough reason to marry,' he said firmly, loudly, his voice shaking her so she flinched, and he groaned. 'Damn it, India, this isn't enough for you. Any fool can see you deserve better than what I can give you. This marriage was a mistake, but, fortunately, not one I will live to regret.'

Pain seared her. She stared at him, struggling to draw breath.

'I will take legal advice on the line of succession,' he said quietly. 'As I should have done from the beginning. I understand the importance of ensuring their birthright. If needs be, we may marry purely for their birth, and dissolve the marriage almost immediately. I appreciate that is still far from ideal—'

'Stop.' Anger shifted through her; the word emerged as a roar. 'Just, stop this.'

Surprised by her outburst, he did so.

'You just said you persuaded me into this marriage, rather than giving me any real choice, and now you're doing exactly the same thing about cancelling our marriage. Don't you care what I want?'

'All I care about is what you want!' he responded with strange determination, so an odd, uncertain suspicion began to flicker to life in the recesses of her brain.

'And you think I want this?'

'Yes. Clearly.'

'Why is it clear?'

'Because I can see the fear in your eyes. The hesitation in your steps. A bride should glow with pleasure, and you do not.' He moved closer and she sucked in a deep breath, bracing for his nearness. 'You deserve to marry a man who makes you glow.'

'And how will you feel then, Khalil?'

He stopped walking and stared at her, his eyes a stormy grey with flecks of gold showing uncertainty.

'If we don't marry now, and in a year's time I meet someone else. How will you feel?'

'Relieved,' he said, but that flicker of doubt burst into a full flame. Her heart began to pound.

'Oh, yeah?' she whispered. 'Then why do I only see fear in your face? Is that what all this is about, Khalil? You're afraid?'

He stared down at her, his nostrils flaring. 'Of what?'

'Of loving me! Loving someone is an act of faith. You have to trust them not to hurt you, and Fatima betrayed that trust, so you're afraid to trust me, even though you know I'm different. But more than that—and here's what you really need to understand—loving someone isn't a choice. Do you think you can end our engagement and whatever feelings are in here—' she jabbed her finger into his chest '—will simply go away? Do you think you'll stop thinking about me? Do you think you'll stop wanting me?'

'I think you'll be happy.'

'I won't be, because you're the man I love. Like

I said, it's not a choice. I can't simply box away those feelings and move on to some other guy. I don't *want* to move on.'

'Even if I can never give you what you want?'

Flames overtook her. 'Oh, Khalil, you *can* give it to me. In fact, you already have. What you've done just now is incontrovertible proof—not just of your decency, but of your love for me. You care about me—to the point you'd break with your constitution to ensure my happiness. What is that if not love?'

'Respect,' he muttered. 'Fairness.'

Sadness washed over her. She knew she was right, but he was determined to fight her. 'Are you really so afraid of this?' she said gently, because now her pain was a shared pain.

'If I'm afraid, it's of hurting you. Of seeing you live a lifetime, broken by our marriage. I cannot bear it.'

'And why do you think that is?' She allowed the rhetorical question to fall between them, watching him, waiting for him to speak. He didn't, and the weight of his silence grew heavier and heavier until India sighed, tears stinging her eyes. 'Is this really what you want?'

He stared at her, a pulse working overtime at his temple. 'It's the right thing to do.'

She nodded, a single tear falling down her

cheek. She brushed it away quickly. 'That's strange, because it feels the opposite of right, doesn't it?'

She stared at him for a moment, waiting for an answer that didn't come, and then, on a huge gasp of air, spun away, moving back to the heavy wooden doors. She wrenched them open and startled to see Astrid in a close conversation with Khalil's parents, across the room. For a moment, she stood perfectly still, pale-faced and frozen to the spot, and then she turned, moving quickly away from them, away from the flower-embellished altar at the head of the room, back to the golden doors that had marked her entrance to the ceremony.

Her breath was burning, coming in shallow spurts, just as it had before, but this was for another reason. She wasn't panicking now, so much as struggling to get enough oxygen—grief had swollen inside her, forming an organ of sadness, and it had overtaken the space previously occupied by her lungs. Once she'd cleared the room, she broke into a run, lifting the heavy silk skirts of her dress, holding back a sob until she'd rounded the corner. Then, she pressed her back to the wall and gave into her tears, letting them fall unchecked, perfectly aware in that moment she'd never know true happiness again.

* * *

He swore to himself as he followed her, ignoring his father's commands that he stop, his mother's pleas for him to come back and explain himself. He was aware, vaguely, of Astrid's hushed tones urging patience and calm, but nothing—no one—could prevent him from going after India. Hell. He'd wanted to fix things for her, to make her happy, and he'd failed miserably.

He cursed again as he came out of the Court Rooms and looked left and right, the empty corridors filling him with a sense of panic and dread that defied logic. He knew she couldn't leave the palace without his knowledge and consent—a fact that filled his mouth with tart acidity, for what that said about her living conditions this past month. She'd been his virtual prisoner, and still she believed she *wanted* to marry him?

He thrust his hands onto his hips and looked left once more, but this time, a palace guard caught his eye and with the simplest shift of his head nodded further down the corridor, and around a corner. Khalil stood right where he was for all of two seconds and then moved quickly, his long legs carrying him with haste through the ancient hallways and then to the left.

And when he saw her, his heart ceased to function as he'd known it. It no longer beat, but burst.

It was no simple organ in his body, but a creation of something more, something that was intrinsically linked to India. Seeing her in tears immediately pulled at him, so he groaned, striding towards her so fast she didn't realise he was there until he put his hands beneath her elbows and drew her to him, pressing her sobbing body to his. She was stiff, resisting him at first, and his heart squeezed again, recognising her rejection and knowing it was the least he deserved.

But he moved a hand to her back, stroking her there, each touch lighting a part of him with intuition and understanding—an understanding he would never have found if India had been less courageous, and less wise. She'd been prepared to fight him—to fight for him—even when he'd pushed her away again and again with his stubborn insistence that she meant nothing to him. He couldn't even imagine how ferociously she would fight for their children!

His heart swelled to overtake his whole body and he pulled away from her just far enough to look into her eyes for several long, vital seconds.

'You're right,' he said finally, moving his hands to cup her face, loving the feel of her there, the goodness and beauty and wisdom and strength that fired through her eyes filling him with all the strength he needed to face the truth. 'I love you. And the idea of that terrifies me. But a life without you in it scares me so much more—a fact I didn't fully appreciate until I watched you walk away from me just now. My God, India, how did you do this to me? Somehow, when I was not paying attention, you dug in here and I know now that you will always be there—a part of me. The best part of me.'

Her lips parted and her eyes, awash with sadness, met his. 'I don't know why you're saying this. If it's because you feel bad, please don't. I always, always appreciate honesty—'

'Then I am glad I can finally give that to you. In my defence, I have not been honest with myself either. I fought this so hard. I wanted to keep you in a neat little box, a wife of convenience who would never mean more to me—yes, I hear how absurd and stupid that is, after everything we've shared. And it is not, in any way, something I could ever have achieved with you, my darling, beautiful India.'

She blinked, each flutter of her lashes seeming to clear the sadness away. He expelled a breath he hadn't realised he'd been holding, releasing tension and pent-up angst from deep within his gut. She sparkled once more. But there was still something in the depths of her gaze that held him back. He hadn't convinced her yet.

'But this wedding today is still wrong,' he said gently. 'I do not want to marry you in a hushed, hurried affair. When—if—we marry, it should be worthy of the love I feel for you.'

Her eyes flashed away from him. 'I'm not Fatima,' she said firmly. 'I don't *want* a big wedding. That's never been what this is about.'

'Not a big wedding, no, but a wedding that celebrates our love, with our loved ones present. All of them. How can we marry without your brother here, India? Without me even having met someone who is so important to you?'

Her gaze flickered back to his, and his heart soared. He could see that he'd expressed a hesitation she herself felt.

'But it's more than that.' He scanned her face slowly. 'I do not want to marry you until you believe the truth of my words. When you walk down the aisle towards me, I want you to be floating on air. I want you to glow with happiness and certainty. I want you to glow with the knowledge of my love for you and trust in you.' He caught her hands in his, lifting them between their bodies. 'I love you. I have loved you, I think, for as long as I've known you, since I first saw you. I knew I wanted to make you mine, but it was so much more than physical. I felt that if I didn't take you home that night, a part of me would wither into nothingness. And then, that night we shared was like something out of time and reality. It was like a dream. You were unlike any woman I had ever known.'

'Until the morning…'

'And I reacted so harshly, because already you had come to mean so much to me. I think, if I was truly honest with myself, I would admit that a part of me had begun to build a fantasy about our future. So when Ethan told me such a vile lie about you, I clung to it, because it was proof of something I'd come to believe—not about you but about love, lies, and about all women.'

'You were protecting yourself,' she whispered softly, her heart so gentle even then that she rose to his defence.

'That doesn't make it okay. I pride myself on my instincts and, with you, I had it so completely wrong. If you had not conceived the twins, I shudder to think of what I might have lost.'

'Might have?' she said with a lifted brow.

'You have no idea how I had to fight from coming back to New York. I thought about you, India. I thought about you often. You were like a fever in my bloodstream and I have no doubt I would have realised, at some point, that things between us were unresolved. If only I could have realised that I loved you—imagine how much simpler this would have been.'

'Simpler, perhaps, but do you know, Khalil, I'm not sure I would change a thing about what we've shared. Our love has been forged in fire, tested at many points, and I know, without a shadow of a doubt, that it's the kind of love that will survive anything. Anything. So long as we live, and love—'

'And trust,' he finished, dropping his forehead to hers before brushing their lips together.

Thirty minutes later, after more reflecting on their love, and the circumstances that had brought them to it, they returned to the Court Rooms, hand in hand.

The three guests were still there, and as the doors opened they turned, as one, to the couple.

'The wedding is off,' Khalil said, with a broad grin, which brought a corresponding frown to the faces of his parents and Astrid.

'What? Why?' Astrid looked from one to the other.

'Because, my dear cousin, when you love someone with your whole heart, as I do India, it is not enough to marry like this. I want to shout it from the rooftops. I want a wedding that the whole kingdom hears of.' He turned to face India then, his voice ever so slightly uneven. 'I want everyone in the world to know that I have fallen in love with the woman I intend to spend the rest of my life attempting to deserve.' He squeezed India's hand, before turning back to Astrid. 'And we will count on you to help us organise it.'

Astrid beamed as she swept towards them, pulling India into her arms in an enormous hug. 'Of course! This is a far better idea, cousin. I'm glad you are not completely brainless after all.' She drew back and winked at India, in time for Khalil's parents to appear.

'Your Highnesses.' India pulled free of Astrid and Khalil and dipped into a low curtsy.

It was Khalil's father who laughed, a gruff noise, before putting a hand on India's forearm. 'My dear girl, please stop that at once.'

She shifted an uncertain glance at Khalil.

'You are to marry our son. You clearly make him happier than we have ever seen him. We're family now. We do not need to stand on ceremony.'

And then, Khalil's mother hugged her, and India fought back more tears, but the kind that were drawn from the happiest wellspring a person could possess. Somehow, she'd found her way to family, to home, and every single part of her was whole again. She smiled, and wondered if she'd ever stop.

EPILOGUE

'YOU COULD SKIP the meeting,' he murmured, squeezing her hand.

India el Abdul slid her husband a sidelong glance. 'And say what? That our two-and-a-half-year-old twins kept me up all night? I don't think that's an excuse anyone will appreciate.'

'Or that the baby in your belly has you running for the bathroom every five minutes,' he said with a sympathetic grimace. Khalil had wished, many times, that he could do more to relieve the burdens of pregnancy, but, beyond running warm baths, offering back massages and foot rubs at any time of day, he was relegated to the role of silent witness.

'It's fine,' she said, patting a hand over her gently rounded stomach. 'I'm looking forward to this. I've worked hard on the proposal.'

'I know you have.' Khalil's face stretched with pride. India's economic forecast for Khatrain was detailed, innovative and, in his opinion, brilliant. But that wasn't just the bias of a doting husband—India had collaborated with economics professors the world over, pulling together a strategy that would take Khatrain forward, not just economically, but in terms of social development too. The investment in schooling and child-care centres meant their people would continue to live in one of the most prosperous and fair countries in the world.

'I'm proud of you,' he said, quietly, as the doors to the economics chamber were opened. India blinked up at him, smiling, a smile that made it appear as though the sun were filtering through her face, warmth and enthusiasm exuded by every pore. 'Almost as proud as my parents are of you.'

She laughed. It was a running joke between them that Khalil's parents loved India more than they did Khalil. They thought she was utterly perfect and could do no wrong. They were also incredibly supportive grandparents, spending as much time as they could with the twins.

'I know you are.' She squeezed his fingers, looking directly forward. 'Thank you.'

He dropped her hand as they entered, purposefully walking a step behind his wife. This was her moment. She had worked hard, channelling her innate abilities and passions into the last eighteen months of work, developing a report that was thorough, achievable and inspired. She deserved every accolade that was laid at her feet.

And though Khalil had expected that to be the case, even he could not have prepared for the rapturous response her report would garner. From even his oldest and most cynical advisors there was only praise, and the room hummed with the kind of enthusiasm he wasn't sure he'd seen in his lifetime.

'Did that just happen?' India asked, eyes wide, when they were alone again.

Khalil nodded. 'It's fair to say, you were a hit.'

India laughed, relieved. 'I knew the report was good, but I hadn't expected—'

'You deserve it,' he interrupted, brushing his lips to hers. 'I think you are incredible.'

She sighed, lifting up onto the tips of her toes to kiss him back.

'What time is it?' she asked against his lips.

'Just past noon. Why?'

'We have several hours before the dinner.'

She flashed a wide-eyed glance at him, a smile playing about her lips. Jackson was due to fly in that afternoon, and, as per their tradition, that meant a big, happy dinner with all of them— Khalil and India, Khalil's parents, Astrid, the twins, and Jackson. It was always loud, fun, with a lot of lively conversation about anything from politics to Broadway shows and economics initiatives.

'Then I guess we'll have to think of a way to kill time.'

'Exactly what I was thinking. Do you have any ideas…?'

He pulled back, a smile crossing his lips as he saw the glint in his wife's eyes. 'Many, many ideas,' he said with mock seriousness, earning a pout from her.

'Such as?'

He scooped down and lifted her easily, cradling her to his chest. 'Plans that are better discussed anywhere but here.'

'Like our bedroom?'

'The perfect venue, Your Highness.'

She laughed as they swept from the room, the bright afternoon sunshine crossing their paths like a golden blade, bathing them in warmth and optimism, paving the way for a future that would be blessed. Light shone, and love grew, as it always would.

* * * * *